Horror, Murder and the Macabre in France

Classic Writers such as Bram Stoker, Gaston Leroux and Montague Summers Pen Short Stories of Terror set in France

British Library Cataloguing-in-Publication Data
A catalogue record for this book is available from
the British Library

CONTENTS

THE BURIAL OF THE RATS

Bram Stoker

*　　*　　*

Leaving Paris by the Orleans road, cross the Enceinte, and, turning to the right, you find yourself in a somewhat wild and not at all savoury district. Right and left, before and behind, on every side rise great heaps of dust and waste accumulated by the process of time.

Paris has its night as well as its day life, and the sojourner who enters his hotel in the rue de Rivoli or the rue St. Honoré late at night or leaves it early in the morning, can guess, in coming near Montrouge – if he has not done so already – the purpose of those great wagons that look like boilers on wheels which he finds halting everywhere as he passes.

Every city has its peculiar institutions created out of its own needs; and one of the most notable institutions of Paris is its rag-picking population. In the early morning – and Parisian life commences at an early hour – may be seen in most streets, standing on the pathway opposite every court and alley and between every few houses, as still in some American cities, even in parts of New York, large wooden boxes into which the domestics or tenement-holders empty the accumulated dust of the past day. Round these boxes gather and pass on, when the work is done, to fresh fields of labour and pastures new, squalid hungry-looking men and women, the implements of whose craft consist of a coarse bag or basket slung over the shoulder and a little rake with which they turn over and probe and examine in the minutest manner the dustbins. They pick up and deposit in their baskets, by aid of their rakes, whatever they may find, with the same facility as a Chinaman uses his chopsticks.

Paris is a city of centralization – and centralization and classification are closely allied. In the early times, when centralization is becoming a fact, its forerunner is classification. All things which are similar or analogous become grouped together, and from the grouping of groups rises one whole or central point. We see radiating many long arms with innumerable tentaculae, and in the centre rises a gigantic head with a comprehensive brain and keen eyes to look on every side and ears sensitive to hear – and a voracious mouth to swallow.

Other cities resemble all the birds and beasts and fishes whose appetites and digestions are normal. Paris alone is the analogical apotheosis of the octopus. Product of centralization carried to an *ad absurdum*. It fairly represents the devil fish; and in no respects is the resemblance more curious than in the similarity of the digestive apparatus.

Those intelligent tourists who, having surrendered their individuality into the hands of Messrs. Cook or Gaze, 'do' Paris in three days, are often puzzled to know how it is that the dinner which in London would cost about six shillings, can be had for three francs in a café in the Palais Royal. They need have no more wonder if they will but consider the classification which is a theoretic speciality of Parisian life, and adopt all round the fact from which the chiffonier has his genesis.

The Paris of 1850 was not like the Paris of today, and those who see the Paris of Napoleon and Baron Haussman can hardly realize the existence of the state of things forty-five years ago.

Among other things, however, which have not changed are those districts where the waste is gathered. Dust is dust all the world over, in every age, and the family likeness of dust heaps is perfect. The traveller, therefore, who visits the environs of Montrouge can go back in fancy without difficulty to the year 1850.

In this year I was making a prolonged stay in Paris. I was very much in love with a young lady who, though she returned my passion, so far yielded to the wishes of her parents that she had promised not to see me or to correspond with me for a year. I, too, had been compelled to accede to these conditions under a vague hope of parental approval. During the term of probation I had promised to remain out

3

of the country and not to write to my dear one until the expiration of the year.

Naturally the time went heavily with me. There was not one of my own family or circle who could tell me of Alice, and none of her own folk had, I am sorry to say, sufficient generosity to send me even an occasional word of comfort regarding her health and well-being. I spent six months wandering about Europe, but as I could find no satisfactory distraction in travel, I determined to come to Paris, where, at least, I would be within easy hail of London in case any good fortune should call me thither before the appointed time. That 'hope deferred maketh the heart sick' was never better exemplified than in my case, for in addition to the perpetual longing to see the face I loved there was always with me a harrowing anxiety lest some accident should prevent me showing Alice in due time that I had, throughout the long period of probation, been faithful to her trust and my own love. Thus, every adventure which I undertook had a fierce pleasure of its own, for it was fraught with possible consequences greater than it would have ordinarily borne.

Like all travellers I exhausted the places of most interest in the first month of my stay, and was driven in the second month to look for amusement whithersoever I might. Having made sundry journeys to the better-known suburbs, I began to see that there was a *terra incognita*, in so far as the guide book was concerned, in the social wilderness lying between these attractive points. Accordingly I began to systematize my researches, and each day took up the thread of my exploration at the place where I had on the previous day dropped it.

In the process of time my wanderings led me near Montrouge, and I saw that hereabouts lay the Ultima Thule of social exploration – a country as little known as that round the source of the White Nile. And so I determined to investigate philosophically the chiffonier – his habitat, his life, and his means of life.

The job was an unsavoury one, difficult of accomplishment, and with little hope of adequate reward. However,

4

despite reason, obstinacy prevailed, and I entered into my new investigation with a keener energy than I could have summoned to aid me in any investigation leading to any end, valuable or worthy.

One day, late in a fine afternoon, toward the end of September, I entered the holy of holies of the city of dust. The place was evidently the recognized abode of a number of chiffoniers, for some sort of arrangement was manifested in the formation of the dust heaps near the road. I passed amongst these heaps, which stood like orderly sentries, determined to penetrate further and trace dust to its ultimate location.

As I passed along I saw behind the dust heaps a few forms that flitted to and fro, evidently watching with interest the advent of any stranger to such a place. The district was like a small Switzerland, and as I went forward my tortuous course shut out the path behind me.

Presently I got into what seemed a small city or community of chiffoniers. There were a number of shanties or huts, such as may be met with in the remote parts of the Bog of Allan – rude places with wattled walls, plastered with mud and roofs of rude thatch made from stable refuse – such places as one would not like to enter for any consideration, and which even in water-colour could only look picturesque if judiciously treated. In the midst of these huts was one of the strangest adaptations – I cannot say habitations – I had ever seen. An immense old wardrobe, the colossal remnant of some boudoir of Charles VII, or Henry II, had been converted into a dwelling-house. The double doors lay open, so that the entire ménage was open to public view. In the open half of the wardrobe was a common sitting-room of some four feet by six, in which sat, smoking their pipes round a charcoal brazier, no fewer than six old soldiers of the First Republic, with their uniforms torn and worn threadbare. Evidently they were of the *mauvais sujet* class; their bleary eyes and limp jaws told plainly of a common love of absinthe; and their eyes had that haggard, worn look of slumbering ferocity which follows hard in the wake of drink.

The other side stood as of old, with its shelves intact, save that they were cut to half their depth, and in each shelf of which there were six, was a bed made with rags and straw. The half-dozen of worthies who inhabited this structure looked at me curiously as I passed; and when I looked back after going a little way I saw their heads together in a whispered conference. I did not like the look of this at all, for the place was very lonely, and the men looked very, very villainous. However, I did not see any cause for fear, and went on my way, penetrating further and further into the Sahara. The way was tortuous to a degree, and from going round in a series of semi-circles, as one goes in skating with the Dutch roll, I got rather confused with regard to the points of the compass.

When I had penetrated a little way I saw, as I turned the corner of a half-made heap, sitting on a heap of straw an old soldier with threadbare coat.

'Hallo!' said I to myself; 'the First Republic is well represented here in its soldiery.'

As I passed him the old man never even looked up at me, but gazed on the ground with stolid persistency. Again I remarked to myself: 'See what a life of rude warfare can do! This old man's curiosity is a thing of the past.'

When I had gone a few steps, however, I looked back suddenly, and saw that curiosity was not dead, for the veteran had raised his head and was regarding me with a very queer expression. He seemed to me to look very like one of the six worthies in the press. When he saw me looking he dropped his head; and without thinking further of him I went on my way, satisfied that there was a strange likeness between these old warriors.

Presently I met another old soldier in a similar manner. He, too, did not notice me whilst I was passing.

By this time it was getting late in the afternoon, and I began to think of retracing my steps. Accordingly I turned to go back, but could see a number of tracks leading between different mounds and could not ascertain which of them I should take. In my perplexity I wanted to see someone of whom to ask the way, but could see no one. I determined to go on a few mounds further and so try to see someone – not a veteran.

I gained my object, for after going a couple of hundred yards I saw before me a single shanty such as I had seen before – with, however, the difference that this was not one for living in, but merely a roof with three walls open in front. From the evidences which the neighbourhood exhibited I took it to be a place for sorting. Within it was an old woman wrinkled and bent with age; I approached her to ask the way.

She rose as I came close and I asked her my way. She immediately commenced a conversation; and it occurred to me that here in the very centre of the Kingdom of Dust was the place to gather details of the history of Parisian rag-picking – particularly as I could do so from the lips of one who looked like the oldest inhabitant.

I began my inquiries, and the old woman gave me most interesting answers – she had been one of the ceteuces who sat daily before the guillotine and had taken an active part among the women who signalized themselves by their violence in the revolution. While we were talking she said suddenly: 'But m'sieur must be tired standing,' and dusted a rickety old stool for me to sit down. I hardly liked to do so for many reasons; but the poor old woman was so civil that I did not like to run the risk of hurting her by refusing, and moreover the conversation of one who had been at the taking of the Bastille was so interesting that I sat down and so our conversation went on.

While we were talking an old man – older and more bent and wrinkled even than the woman – appeared from behind the shanty. 'Here is Pierre,' said she. 'M'sieur can hear stories now if he wishes, for Pierre was in everything, from the Bastille to Waterloo.' The old man took another stool at my request and we plunged into a sea of revolutionary reminiscences. This old man, albeit clothed like a scarecrow, was like any one of the six veterans.

I was now sitting in the centre of the low hut with the woman on my left hand and the man on my right, each of them being somewhat in front of me. The place was full of all sorts of curious objects of lumber, and of many things that I wished far away. In one corner was a heap of rags which seemed to move from the number of vermin it contained, and in the other a heap of bones whose odour was something shocking. Every now and then, glancing at the heaps, I could see the gleaming eyes of some of the rats which infested the place. These loathsome objects were bad enough, but what looked even more dreadful was an old butcher's axe with an iron handle stained with clots of blood leaning up against the wall on the right hand side. Still, these things did not give me much concern. The talk of the two old people was so fascinating that I stayed on and on, till the evening came and the dust heaps threw dark shadows over the vales between them.

After a time I began to grow uneasy. I could not tell how or why, but somehow I did not feel satisfied. Uneasiness is an instinct and means warning. The psychic faculties are often the sentries of the intellect, and when they sound the alarm reason begins to act, although perhaps not consciously.

This was so with me. I began to bethink me where I was and by what surrounded, and to wonder how I should fare in case I should be attacked; and then the thought suddenly burst upon me, although without any overt cause, that I was in danger. Prudence whispered: 'Be still and make no sign,' and so I was still and made no sign, for I knew that four cunning eyes were on me. 'Four eyes – if not more.' My God, what a horrible thought! The whole shanty might be surrounded on three sides with villains! I might be in the midst of a band of such desperadoes as only half a century of periodic revolution can produce.

With a sense of danger my intellect and observation quickened, and I grew more watchful than was my wont. I noticed that the old woman's eyes were constantly wandering towards my hands. I looked at them too, and saw the cause – my rings. On my left little finger I had a large signet and on the right a good diamond.

I thought that if there was any danger my first care was to avert suspicion. Accordingly I began to work the conversation round to rag-picking – to the drains – of the things found there; and so by easy stages to jewels. Then, seizing a favourable opportunity, I asked the old woman if she knew anything of such things. She answered that she did a little. I held out my right hand, and, showing her the diamond, asked her what she thought of that. She answered that her eyes were bad, and stooped over my hand. I said as nonchalantly as I could: 'Pardon me! You will see better thus!' and taking it off handed it to her. An unholy light came into her withered old face, as she touched it. She stole one glance at me swift and keen as a flash of lightning.

She bent over the ring for a moment, her face quite concealed as though examining it. The old man looked straight out of the front of the shanty before him, at the same time fumbling in his pockets and producing a screw of tobacco in a paper and a pipe, which he proceeded to fill. I took advantage of the pause and the momentary rest from the searching eyes on my face to look carefully round the place, now dim and shadowy in the gloaming. There still lay all the heaps of varied reeking foulness; there the terrible bloodstained axe leaning against the wall in the right-hand corner, and everywhere, despite the gloom, the baleful glitter of the eyes of the rats. I could see them even through some of the chinks of the boards at the back low down close to the ground. But stay! these latter eyes seemed more than usually large and bright and baleful!

For an instant my heart stood still, and I felt in that whirling condition of mind in which one feels a sort of spiritual drunkenness, and as though the body is only maintained erect in that there is no time for it to fall before recovery. Then, in another second, I was calm – coldly calm, with all my energies in full vigour, with a self-control which I felt to be perfect and with all my feeling and instincts alert.

Now I knew the full extent of my danger: I was watched and surrounded by desperate people! I could not even guess at how many of them were lying there on the ground behind the shanty, waiting for the moment to strike. I knew that I was big and strong, and they knew it, too. They knew also, as I did, that I was an Englishman and would make a fight for it; and so we waited. I had, I felt, gained an advantage in the last few seconds, for I knew my danger and understood the situation. Now, I thought, is the test of my courage – the enduring test: the fighting test may come later!

The old woman raised her head and said to me in a satisfied kind of way:

'A very fine ring, indeed – a beautiful ring! Oh, me! I once had such rings, plenty of them, and bracelets and earrings! Oh! for in those fine days I led the town a dance! But they've forgotten me now! They've forgotten me! They? Why they never heard of me! Perhaps their grandfathers remember me, some of them!' and she laughed a harsh, croaking laugh. And then I am bound to say that she astonished me, for she handed me back the ring with a certain suggestion of old-fashioned grace which was not without its pathos.

The old man eyed her with a sort of sudden ferocity, half rising from his stool, and said to me suddenly and hoarsely:

'Let me see!'

I was about to hand the ring when the old woman said:

'No! no, do not give it to Pierre! Pierre is eccentric. He loses things; and such a pretty ring!'

'Cat!' said the old man, savagely. Suddenly the old woman said, rather more loudly than was necessary:

'Wait! I shall tell you something about a ring.' There was something in the sound of her voice that jarred upon me. Perhaps it was my hyper-sensitiveness, wrought up as I was to such a pitch of nervous excitement, but I seemed to think that she was not addressing me. As I stole a glance round the place I saw the eyes of the rats in the bone heaps, but missed the eyes along the back. But even as I looked I saw them again appear. The old woman's 'Wait!' had given me a respite from attack, and the men had sunk back to their reclining posture.

'I once lost a ring – a beautiful diamond hoop that had belonged to a queen, and which was given to me by a farmer of the taxes, who afterwards cut his throat because I sent him away. I thought it must have been stolen, and taxed my people; but I could get no trace. The police came and suggested that it had found its way to the drain. We descended – I in my fine clothes, for I would not trust them with my beautiful ring! I know more of the drains since then, and of rats, too! but I shall never forget the horror of that place – alive with blazing eyes, a wall of them just outside the light of our torches. Well, we got beneath my house. We searched the outlet of the drain, and there in the filth found my ring, and we came out.

'But we found something else also before we came! As we were coming towards the opening a lot of sewer rats – human ones this time – came towards us. They told the police that one of their number had gone into the drain, but had not returned. He had gone in only shortly before we had, and, if lost, could hardly be far off. They asked help to seek him, so we turned back. They tried to prevent me going, but I insisted. It was a new excitement, and had I not recovered my ring? Not far did we go till we came on something. There was but little water, and the bottom of the drain was raised with brick, rubbish, and much matter of the kind. He had made a fight for it, even when his torch had gone out. But they were too many for him! They had not been long about it! The bones were still warm; but they were picked clean. They had even eaten their own dead ones and there were bones of rats as well as of the man. They took it cool enough those other – the human ones – and joked of their comrade when they found him dead, though they would have helped him living. Bah! what matters it – life or death?'

'And had you no fear?' I asked her.

'Fear!' she said with a laugh. 'Me have fear? Ask Pierre! But I was younger then, and, as I came through that horrible

11

drain with its wall of greedy eyes, always moving with the circle of the light from the torches, I did not feel easy. I kept on before the men, though! It is a way I have! I never let the men get it before me. All I want is a chance and a means! And they ate him up – took every trace away except the bones; and no one knew it, nor no sound of him was ever heard!' Here she broke into a chuckling fit of the ghastliest merriment which it was ever my lot to hear and see. A great poetess describes her heroine singing: 'Oh! to see or hear her singing! Scarce I knew which is the divinest.'

And I can apply the same idea to the old crone – in all save the divinity, for I scarce could tell which was the most hellish – the harsh, malicious, satisfied, cruel laugh, or the leering grin, and the horrible square opening of the mouth like a tragic mask, and the yellow gleam of the few discoloured teeth in the shapeless gums. In that laugh and with that grin and the chuckling satisfaction I knew as well as if it had been spoken to me in words of thunder that my murder was settled, and the murderers only bided the proper time for its accomplishment. I could read between the lines of her gruesome story the commands to her accomplices. 'Wait,' she seemed to say, 'bide your time. I shall strike the first blow. Find the weapon for me, and I shall make the opportunity! He shall not escape! Keep him quiet, and then no one will be wiser. There will be no outcry, and the rats will do their work!'

It was growing darker and darker; the night was coming. I stole a glance round the shanty, still all the same! The bloody axe in the corner, the heaps of filth, and the eyes on the bone heaps and in the crannies of the floor.

Pierre had been still ostensibly filling his pipe; he now struck a light and began to puff away at it. The old woman said:

'Dear heart, how dark it is! Pierre, like a good lad, light the lamp!'

Pierre got up and with the lighted match in his hand touched the wick of a lamp which hung at one side of the entrance to the shanty, and which had a reflector that threw the light all over the place. It was evidently that which was used for their sorting at night.

'Not that, stupid! Not that! The lantern!' she called out to him.

He immediately blew it out, saying: "All right, mother, I'll find it,' and he hustled about the left corner of the room – the old woman saying through the darkness:

'The lantern; the lantern! Oh! That is the light that is most useful to us poor folk. The lantern was the friend of the revolution! It is the friend of the chiffonier! It helps us when all else fails.'

Hardly had she said the word when there was a kind of creaking of the whole place, and something was steadily dragged over the room.

Again I seemed to read between the lines of her words. I knew the lesson of the lantern.

'One of you get on the roof with a noose and strangle him as he passes out if we fail within.'

As I looked out the opening I saw the loop of a rope outlined black against the lurid sky. I was now, indeed, beset.

Pierre was not long in finding the lantern. I kept my eyes fixed through the darkness on the old woman. Pierre struck his light, and by its flash I saw the old woman raise from the ground beside her where it had mysteriously appeared, and then hide in the folds of her gown, a long sharp knife or dagger. It seemed to be like a butcher's sharpening iron fined to a keen point.

The lantern was lit.

'Bring it here, Pierre,' she said. 'Place it in the doorway where we can see it. See how nice it is! It shuts out the darkness from us; it is just right!'

Just right for her and her purposes! It threw all its light on my face, leaving in gloom the faces of both Pierre and the woman, who sat outside of me on each side.

I felt that the time of action was approaching; but I knew now that the first signal and movement would come from the woman, and so watched her.

I was all unarmed, but I had made up my mind what to do. At the first movement I would seize the butcher's axe in the right-hand corner and fight my way out. At least, I would die hard. I stole a glance round to fix its exact locality so that I could not fail to seize it at the first effort, for then, if ever, time and accuracy would be precious.

Good God! It was gone! All the horror of the situation burst upon me; but the bitterest thought of all was that if the issue of the terrible position should be against me Alice would infallibly suffer. Either she would believe me false – and any lover, or any one who has ever been one, can imagine the bitterness of the thought – or else she would go on loving long after I had been lost to her and to the world, so that her life would be broken and embittered, shattered with disappointment and despair. The very magnitude of the pain braced me up and nerved me to bear the dread scrutiny of the plotters.

I think I did not betray myself. The old woman was watching me as a cat does a mouse; she had her right hand hidden in the folds of her gown, clutching, I knew, that long, cruel-looking dagger. Had she seen any disappointment in my face she would, I felt, have known that the moment had come, and would have sprung on me like a tigress, certain of taking me unprepared.

I looked out into the night, and there I saw new cause for danger. Before and around the hut were at a little distance some shadowy forms; they were quite still, but I knew that they were all alert and on guard. Small chance for me now in that direction.

Again I stole a glance round the place. In moments of great excitement and of great danger, which is excitement, the mind works very quickly, and the keenness of the faculties which depend on the mind grows in proportion. I now felt this. In an instant I took in the whole situation. I saw that the axe had been taken through a small hole made in one of the rotten boards. How rotten they must be to allow of such a thing being done without a particle of noise.

The hut was a regular murder-trap, and was guarded all

around. A garrotter lay on the roof ready to entangle me with his noose if I should escape the dagger of the old hag. In front the way was guarded by I know not how many watchers. And at the back was a row of desperate men – I had seen their eyes still through the crack in the boards of the floor, when last I looked – as they lay prone waiting for the signal to start erect. If it was to be ever, now for it!

As nonchalantly as I could I turned slightly on my stool so as to get my right leg well under me. Then with a sudden jump, turning my head, and guarding it with my hands, and with the fighting instinct of the knights of old, I breathed my lady's name, and hurled myself against the back wall of the hut.

Watchful as they were, the suddenness of my movement surprised both Pierre and the old woman. As I crashed through the rotten timbers I saw the old woman rise with a leap like a tiger and heard her low gasp of baffled rage. My feet lit on something that moved, and as I jumped away I knew that I had stepped on the back of one of the row of men lying on their faces outside the hut. I was torn with nails and splinters, but otherwise unhurt. Breathless I rushed up the mound in front of me, hearing as I went the dull crash of the shanty as it collapsed into a mass.

It was a nightmare climb. The mound, though but low, was awfully steep, and with each step I took the mass of dust and cinders tore down with me and gave way under my feet. The dust rose and choked me; it was sickening, foetid, awful; but my climb was, I felt, for life or death, and I struggled on. The seconds seemed hours; but the few moments I had in starting, combined with my youth and strength, gave me a great advantage, and, though several forms struggled after me in deadly silence which was more dreadful than any sound, I easily reached the top. Since then I have climbed the cone of Vesuvius, and as I struggled up that dreary steep amid the sulphurous fumes the memory of that awful night at Montrouge came back to me so vividly that I almost grew faint.

The mound was one of the tallest in the region of dust,

and as I struggled to the top, panting for breath and with my heart beating like a sledge-hammer, I saw away to my left the dull red gleam of the sky, and nearer still the flashing of lights. Thank God! I knew where I was now and where lay the road to Paris!

For two or three seconds I paused and looked back. My pursuers were still well behind me, but struggling up resolutely, and in deadly silence. Beyond, the shanty was a wreck – a mass of timber and moving forms. I could see it well, for flames were already bursting out; the rags and straw had evidently caught fire from the lantern. Still silence there! Not a sound. These old wretches could die game, anyhow.

I had no time for more than a passing glance, for as I cast an eye round the mound preparatory to making my descent I saw several dark forms rushing round on either side to cut me off on my way. It was now a race for life. They were trying to head me off on my way to Paris, and with the instinct of the moment I dashed down to the right-hand side. I was just in time, for, though I came as it seemed to me down the steep in a few steps, the wary old men who were watching me turned back, and one, as I rushed by into the opening between the two mounds in front, almost struck me a blow with that terrible butcher's axe. There could surely not be two such weapons about!

Then began a really horrible chase. I easily ran ahead of the old men, and even when some younger ones and a few women joined in the hunt I easily distanced them. But I did not know the way, and I could not even guide myself by the light in the sky, for I was running away from it. I had heard that, unless of conscious purpose, hunted men turn always to the left, and so I found it now; and so, I suppose, knew also my pursuers, who were more animals than men, and with cunning or instinct had found out such secrets for themselves: for on finishing a quick spurt, after which I intended to take a moment's breathing space, I suddenly saw ahead of me two or three forms swiftly passing behind a mound to the right.

I was in the spider's web now indeed! But with the thought of this new danger came the resource of the hunted, and so I darted down the next turning to the right. I continued in this direction for some hundred yards, and then, making a turn to the left again, felt certain that I had, at any rate, avoided the danger of being surrounded.

But not of pursuit, for on came the rabble after me, steady, dogged, relentless, and still in grim silence.

In the greater darkness the mounds seemed now to be somewhat smaller than before, although – for the night was closing – they looked bigger in proportion: I was now well ahead of my pursuers, so I made a dart up the mound in front.

Oh joy of joys! I was close to the edge of this inferno of dust heaps. Away behind me the red light of Paris was in the sky, and towering up behind rose the heights of Montmartre – a dim light, with here and there brilliant points like stars.

Restored to vigour in a moment, I ran over the few remaining mounds of decreasing size, and found myself on the level land beyond. Even then, however, the prospect was not inviting. All before me was dark and dismal, and I had evidently come on one of those dank, low-lying waste places which are found here and there in the neighbourhood of great cities. Places of waste and desolation, where the space is required for the ultimate agglomeration of all that is noxious, and the ground is so poor as to create no desire of occupancy even in the lowest squatter. With eyes accustomed to the gloom of the evening, and away now from the shadows of those dreadful dust heaps, I could see much more easily than I could a little while ago. It might have been, of course, that the glare in the sky of the lights of Paris, though the city was some miles away, was reflected here. Howsoever it was, I saw well enough to take bearings for certainly some little distance around me.

In front was a bleak, flat waste that seemed almost dead level, with here and there the dark shimmering of stagnant pools. Seemingly far off on the right, amid a small cluster of scattered lights, rose a dark mass of Fort Montrouge, and away to the left in the dim distance, pointed with stray gleams from cottage windows, the lights in the sky showed the locality of Bicêtre. A moment's thought decided me to take to the right and try to reach Montrouge. There at least would be some sort of safety, and I might possibly long before come on some of the cross roads which I knew. Somewhere, not far off, must lie the strategic road made to connect the outlying chain of forts circling the city.

Then I looked back. Coming over the mounds, and outlined black against the glare of the Parisian horizon, I saw several moving figures, and still a long way to the right several more deploying out between me and my destination. They evidently meant to cut me off in this direction, and so my choice became constricted; it lay now between going straight ahead or turning to the left. Stooping to the ground, so as to get the advantage of the horizon as a line of sight, I looked carefully in this direction, but could detect no sign of my enemies. I argued that as they had not guarded or were not trying to guard that point, there was evidently danger to me there already. So I made up my mind to go straight on before me.

It was not an inviting prospect, and as I went on the reality grew worse. The ground became soft and oozy, and now and again gave way beneath me in a sickening kind of way. I seemed somehow to be going down, for I saw round me places seemingly more elevated than where I was, and this in a place which from a little way back seemed dead level. I looked around, but could see none of my pursuers. This was strange, for all along these birds of the night had followed me through the darkness as well as though it was broad daylight. How I blamed myself for coming out in my light-coloured tourist suit of tweed. The silence, and my not being able to see my enemies, whilst I felt that they were watching me, grew appalling, and in the hope of someone not of this ghastly crew hearing me I raised my voice and shouted several times. There was not the slightest response; not even an echo rewarded my efforts. For a while I stood stock still and kept my eyes in one direction. On one of the rising places around me I saw something dark move along, then another, and another. This was to my left, and seemingly moving to head me off.

I thought that again I might with my skill as a runner elude my enemies at this game, and so with all my speed darted forward.

Splash!

My feet had given way in a mass of slimy rubbish, and I had fallen headlong into a reeking, stagnant pool. The water and the mud in which my arms sank up to the elbows was filthy and nauseous beyond description, and in the suddenness of my fall I had actually swallowed some of the filthy stuff, which nearly choked me, and made me gasp for breath. Never shall I forget the moments during which I stood trying to recover myself almost fainting from the foetid odour of the filthy pool, whose white mist rose ghostlike around. Worst of all, with the acute despair of the hunted animal when he sees the pursuing pack closing on him, I saw before my eyes whilst I stood helpless the dark forms of my pursuers moving swiftly to surround me.

It is curious how our minds work on odd matters, even when the energies of thought are seemingly concentrated on some terrible and pressing need. I was in momentary peril of my life: my safety depended on my action, and my choice of alternatives coming now with almost every step I took, and yet I could not but think of the strange dogged persistency of these old men. Their silent resolution, their steadfast, grim, persistency even in such a cause commanded, as well as fear, even a measure of respect. What must they have been in the vigour of their youth. I could understand now that whirlwind rush on the bridge of Arcola, that scornful exclamation of the Old Guard at Waterloo! Unconscious cerebration has its own pleasures, even at such moments; but fortunately it does not in any way clash with the thought from which action springs.

I realized at a glance that so far as I was defeated in my object, my enemies as yet had won. They had succeeded in surrounding me on three sides, and were bent on driving me off to the left hand, where there was already some danger

for me, for they had left no guard. I accepted the alternative
– it was a case of Hobson's choice and run. I had to keep
to the lower ground, for my pursuers were on the higher
places. However, though the ooze and broken ground im-
peded me my youth and training made me able to hold my
ground, and by keeping a diagonal line I not only kept them
from gaining on me but even began to out distance them.
This gave me new heart and strength, and by this time habi-
tual training was beginning to tell and my second wind had
come. Before me the ground rose slightly. I rushed up the
slope and found before me a waste of watery slime, with a
low dyke or bank looking black and grim beyond. I felt that
if I could but reach that dyke in safety I could there, with
solid ground under my feet and some kind of path to guide
me, find with comparative ease a way out of my troubles.
After a glance right and left and seeing no one near, I kept
my eyes for a few minutes to their rightful work of aiding
my feet whilst I crossed the swamp. It was rough, hard
work, but there was little danger, merely toil; and a short
time took me to the dyke. I rushed up the slope exulting; but
here again I met a new shock. On either side of me rose a
number of crouching figures. From right and left they
rushed at me. Each body held a rope.

The cordon was nearly complete. I could pass on neither
side, and the end was near.

There was only one chance, and I took it. I hurled myself
across the dyke, and escaping out of the very clutches of my
foes threw myself into the stream.

At any other time I should have thought that water foul
and filthy, but now it was as welcome as the most crystal
stream to the parched traveller. It was a highway of
safety.

My pursuers rushed after me. Had only one of them held
the rope it would have been all up with me, for he could
have entangled me before I had time to swim a stroke; but
the many hands holding it embarrassed and delayed them,
and when the rope struck the water I heard the splash well
behind me. A few minutes' hard swimming took me across

the stream. Refreshed with the immersion and encouraged by the escape. I climbed the dyke in comparative gaiety of spirits.

From the top I looked back. Through the darkness I saw my assailants scattering up and down along the dyke. The pursuit was evidently not ended, and again I had to choose my course. Beyond the dyke where I stood was a wild swampy place very similar to that which I had crossed. I determined to shun such a place, and thought for a moment whether I would take up or down the dyke. I thought I heard a sound – the muffled sound of oars, so I listened, and then shouted.

No response, but the sound ceased. My enemies had evidently got a boat of some kind. As they were on the up side of me I took the down path and began to run. As I passed to the left of where I had entered the water, I heard several splashes, soft and stealthy, like the sound a rat makes as he plunges into the stream, but vastly greater; and as I looked I saw the dark sheen of the water broken by the ripples of several advancing heads. Some of my enemies were swimming the stream also.

And now behind me, up the stream, the silence was broken by the quick rattle and creak of oars; my enemies were in hot pursuit. I put my best leg foremost and ran on. After a break of a couple of minutes I looked back, and by a gleam of light through the ragged clouds I saw several dark forms climbing the bank behind me. The wind had now begun to rise, and the water beside me was ruffled and beginning to break in tiny waves on the bank. I had to keep my eyes pretty well on the ground before me, lest I should stumble, for I knew that to stumble was death. After a few minutes I looked back behind me. On the dyke were only a few dark figures, but crossing the waste, swampy ground were many more. What new danger this portended I did not know – could only guess. Then as I ran it seemed to me that my track kept ever sloping away to the right. I looked up ahead and saw that the river was much wider than before, and that the dyke on which I stood fell quite away, and beyond it was another stream on whose near bank I saw some of the dark forms now across the marsh. I was on an island of some kind.

My situation was now indeed terrible, for my enemies had hemmed me in on every side. Behind came the quickening roll of the oars, as though my pursuers knew that the end was close. Around me on every side was desolation; there was not a roof or light, as far as I could see. Far off to the right rose some dark mass, but what it was I knew not. For a moment I paused to think what I should do, not for more, for my pursuers were drawing closer. Then my mind was made up. I slipped down the bank and took to the water. I struck out straight ahead so as to gain the current by clearing the backwater of the island, for such I presume it was, when I had passed into the stream. I waited till a cloud came driving across the moon and leaving all in darkness. Then I took off my hat and laid it softly on the water floating with the stream, and a second after dived to the right and struck out under water with all my might. I was, I suppose, half a minute under water, and when I rose came up as softly as I could, and turning, looked back. There went my light brown hat floating merrily away. Close behind it came a rickety old boat, driven furiously by a pair of oars. The moon was still partly obscured by the drifting clouds, but in the partial light I could see a man in the bows holding aloft ready to strike what appeared to me to be that same dreadful pole-axe which I had before escaped. As I looked the boat drew closer, closer, and the man struck savagely. The hat disappeared. The man fell forward, almost out of the boat. His comrades dragged him in but without the axe, and then as I turned with all my energies bent on reaching the further bank, I heard the fierce whirr of the muttered 'Sacre!' which marked the anger of my baffled pursuers.

That was the first sound I had heard from human lips during all this dreadful chase, and full as it was of menace and danger to me it was a welcome sound for it broke that awful silence which shrouded and appalled me. It was as though an overt sign that my opponents were men and not ghosts, and that with them I had, at least, the chance of a man, though but one against many,

But now that the spell of silence was broken the sounds came thick and fast. From boat to shore and back from shore to boat came quick question and answer, all in the fiercest whispers. I looked back – a fatal thing to do – for in the instant someone caught sight of my face, which showed white on the dark water, and shouted. Hands pointed to me, and in a moment or two the boat was under way, and following hard after me. I had but a little way to go, but quicker and quicker came the boat after me. A few more strokes and I would be on the shore, but I felt the oncoming of the boat, and expected each second to feel the crash of an oar or other weapon on my head. Had I not seen that dreadful axe disappear in the water I do not think that I could have won the shore. I heard the muttered curses of those not rowing and the laboured breath of the rowers. With one supreme effort for life or liberty I touched the bank and sprang up it. There was not a single second to spare, for hard behind me the boat grounded and several dark forms sprang after me. I gained the top of the dyke, and keeping to the left ran on again. The boat put off and followed down the stream. Seeing this I feared danger in this direction, and quickly turning, ran down the dyke on the other side, and after passing a short stretch of marshy ground gained a wild, open flat country and sped on.

Still behind me came on my relentless pursuers. Far away, below me, I saw the same dark mass as before, but now grown closer and greater. My heart gave a great thrill of delight, for I knew it must be the fortress of Bicêtre, and with new courage I ran on. I had heard that between each and all of the protecting forts of Paris there are strategic ways, deep sunk roads, where soldiers marching should be sheltered from an enemy. I knew that if I could gain this road I would be safe, but in the darkness I could not see any sign of it, so, in blind hope of striking it, I ran on.

Presently I came to the edge of a deep cut, and found

that down below me ran a road guarded on each side by a ditch of water fenced on either side by a straight, high wall.

Getting fainter and dizzier, I ran on; the ground got more broken – more and more still, till I staggered and fell, and rose again, and ran on in the blind anguish of the hunted. Again the thought of Alice nerved me. I would not be lost and wreck her life: I would fight and struggle for life to the bitter end. With a great effort I caught the top of the wall. As, scrambling like a catamount, I drew myself up, I actually felt a hand touch the sole of my foot. I was now on a sort of causeway, and before me I saw a dim light. Blind and dizzy, I ran on, staggered, and fell, rising, covered with dust and blood.

'Halt la!'

The words sounded like a voice from heaven. A blaze of light seemed to enwrap me, and I shouted with joy.

'Qui va la?' The rattle of musketry, the flash of steel before my eyes. Instinctively I stopped, though close behind me came a rush of my pursuers.

Another word or two, and out from a gateway poured, as it seemed to me, a tide of red and blue, as the guard turned out. All around seemed blazing with light, and the flash of steel, the clink and rattle of arms, and the loud, harsh voices of command. As I fell forward, utterly exhausted, a soldier caught me. I looked back in dreadful expectation, and saw the mass of dark forms disappearing into the night. Then I must have fainted. When I recovered my senses I was in the guard room. They gave me brandy, and after a while I was able to tell them something of what had passed. Then a commissary of police appeared, apparently out of the empty air, as is the way of the Parisian police officer. He listened attentively, and then had a moment's consultation with the officer in command. Apparently they were agreed, for they asked me if I were ready now to come with them.

'Where to?' I asked, rising to go.

'Back to the dust heaps. We shall, perhaps, catch them yet!'

'I shall try!' said I.

He eyed me for a moment keenly, and said suddenly: 'Would you like to wait a while or till tomorrow, young Englishman?' This touched me to the quick, as, perhaps, he intended, and I jumped to my feet.

'Come now!' I said; 'now! now! An Englishman is always ready for his duty!'

The commissary was a good fellow, as well as a shrewd one; he slapped my shoulder kindly. 'Brave garçon!' he said. 'Forgive me, but I knew what would do you most good. The guard is ready. Come!'

And so, passing right through the guard room, and through a long vaulted passage, we were out into the night. A few of the men in front had powerful lanterns. Through courtyards and down a sloping way we passed out through a low archway to a sunken road, the same that I had seen in my flight. The order was given to get at the double, and with a quick, springing stride, half run, half walk, the soldiers went swiftly along. I felt my strength renewed again – such is the difference between hunter and hunted. A very short distance took us to a low-lying pontoon bridge across the stream, and evidently very little higher up than I had struck it. Some effort had evidently been made to damage it, for the ropes had all been cut, and one of the chains had been broken. I heard the officer say to the commissary:

'We are just in time! A few more minutes, and they would have destroyed the bridge. Forward, quicker still' and on we went. Again we reached a pontoon on the winding stream; as we came up we heard the hollow boom of the metal drums as the efforts to destroy the bridge was again renewed. A word of command was given, and several men raised their rifles.

'Fire!' A volley rang out. There was a muffled cry, and the dark forms dispersed. But the evil was done, and we saw the far end of the pontoon swing into the stream. This was a serious delay, and it was nearly an hour before we had renewed ropes and restored the bridge sufficiently to allow us to cross.

We renewed the chase. Quicker, quicker we went towards the dust heaps.

After a time we came to a place that I knew. There were the remains of a fire – a few smouldering wood ashes still cast a red glow, but the bulk of the ashes were cold. I knew the site of the hut and the hill behind it up which I had rushed, and in the flickering glow the eyes of the rats still shone with a sort of phosphorescence. The commissary spoke a word to the officer, and he cried:

'Halt!'

The soldiers were ordered to spread around and watch, and then we commenced to examine the ruins. The commissary himself began to lift away the charred boards and rubbish. These the soldiers took and piled together. Presently he started back, then bent down and rising beckoned me.

'See!' he said.

It was a gruesome sight. There lay a skeleton face downwards, a woman by the lines – and old woman by the coarse fibre of the bone. Between the ribs rose a long spike-like dagger made from a butcher's sharpening knife, its keen point buried in the spine.

'You will observe,' said the commissary to the officer and to me as he took out his notebook, 'that the woman must have fallen on her dagger. The rats are many here – see their eyes glistening among that heap of bones – and you will also notice' – I shuddered as he placed his hand on the skeleton – 'that but little time was lost by them, for the bones are scarcely cold!'

There was no other sign of anyone near, living or dead; and so deploying again into line the soldiers passed on. Presently we came to the hut made of the old wardrobe. We approached. In five of the six compartments was an old man sleeping – sleeping so soundly that even the glare of the lanterns did not wake them. Old and grim and grizzled they looked, with their gaunt, wrinkled, bronzed faces and their white moustaches.

The officer called out harshly and loudly a word of command, and in an instant each one of them was on his feet before us and standing at 'attention!'

'What do you here?'

'We sleep,' was the answer.

'Where are the other chiffoniers?' asked the commissary.

'Gone to work.'

'And you?'

'We are on guard!'

'Peste!' laughed the officer grimly, as he looked at the old men one after the other in the face and added with cool deliberate cruelty: 'Asleep on duty! Is this the manner of the Old Guard? No wonder, then, a Waterloo!'

By the gleam of the lantern I saw the grim old faces grow deadly pale, and almost shuddered at the look in the eyes of the old men as the laugh of the soldiers echoed the grim pleasantry of the officer.

I felt in that moment that I was in some measure avenged.

For a moment they looked as though they would throw themselves on the taunter, but years of their life had schooled them and they remained still.

'You are but five,' said the commissary; 'where is the sixth?' The answer came with a grim chuckle.

'He is there!' and the speaker pointed to the bottom of the wardrobe. 'He died last night. You won't find much of him. The burial of the rats is quick!'

The commissary stooped and looked in. Then he turned to the officer and said calmly:

'We may as well go back. No trace here now; nothing to prove that man was the one wounded by your soldiers' bullets! Probably they murdered him to cover up the trace. See!' Again he stooped and placed his hands on the skeleton. 'The rats work quickly and they are many. These bones are warm!'

I shuddered, and so did many more of those around me.

'Form!' said the officer, and so in marching order, with the lanterns swinging in front and the manacled veterans in the midst, with steady tramp we took ourselves out of the dust heaps and turned backward to the fortress of Bicêtre.

My year of probation has long since ended, and Alice is my wife. But when I look back upon that trying twelve month one of the most vivid incidents that memory recalls is that associated with my visit to the City of Dust.

The Other Side

[*a Breton legend*]

COUNT STENBOCK

A la joyeuse Messe noire

'Not that I like it, but one does feel so much better after it – oh, thank you, Mère Yvonne, yes just a little drop more.' So the old crones fell to drinking their hot brandy and water (although of course they only took it medicinally, as a remedy for their rheumatics), all seated round the big fire, and Mère Pinquèle continued her story.

'Oh, yes, then when they get to the top of the hill, there is an altar with six candles quite black and a sort of something in between, that nobody sees quite clearly, and the old black ram with the man's face and long horns begins to say Mass in a sort of gibberish nobody understands, and two black strange things like monkeys glide about with the book and the cruets – arid there's music too, such music. There are things the top half like black cats, and the bottom part like men only their legs are all covered with close black hair, and they play on the bag-pipes, and when they come to the elevation, then – ' Amid the old crones there was lying on the hearth-rug, before the fire, a boy whose large lovely eyes dilated and whose limbs quivered in the very ecstasy of terror.

'Is that all true, Mère Pinquèle?' he said.

'Oh, quite true, and not only that, the best part is yet to come; for they take a child and – ' here Mère Pinquèle showed her fang-like teeth.

'Oh! Mère Pinquèle, are you a witch too?'

'Silence, Gabriel,' said Mère Yvonne, 'how can you say anything so wicked? Why, bless me, the boy ought to have been in bed ages ago.'

Just then all shuddered, and all made the sign of the cross except Mère Pinquèle, for they heard that most dreadful of dreadful sounds –· the howl of a wolf, which begins with three sharp barks and then lifts itself up in a long protracted wail of commingled cruelty and

29

despair, and at last subsides into a whispered growl fraught with eternal malice.

There was a forest and a village and a brook; the village was on one side of the brook, none had dared to cross to the other side. Where the village was, all was green and glad and fertile and fruitful; on the other side the trees never put forth green leaves, and a dark shadow hung over it even at noon-day, and in the night-time one could hear the wolves howling – the werewolves and the wolfmen and the men-wolves, and those very wicked men who for nine days in every year are turned into wolves; but on the green side no wolf was ever seen, and only one little running brook like a silver streak flowed between.

It was spring now and the old crones sat no longer by the fire but before their cottages sunning themselves, and everyone felt so happy that they ceased to tell stories of the 'other side'. But Gabriel wandered by the brook as he was wont to wander, drawn thither by some strange attraction mingled with intense horror.

His schoolfellows did not like Gabriel; all laughed and jeered at him, because he was less cruel and more gentle of nature than the rest; and even as a rare and beautiful bird escaped from a cage is hacked to death by the common sparrows, so was Gabriel among his fellows. Everyone wondered how Mère Yvonne, that buxom and worthy matron, could have produced a son like this, with strange dreamy eyes, who was as they said '*pas comme les autres gamins*'. His only friends were the Abbé Félicien whose Mass he served each morning, and one little girl called Carmeille, who loved him, no-one could make out why.

The sun had already set. Gabriel still wandered by the brook, filled with vague terror and irresistible fascination. The sun set and the moon rose, the full moon, very large and very clear, and the moonlight flooded the forest both this side and the 'other side', and just on the 'other side' of the brook, hanging over, Gabriel saw a large deep blue flower, whose strange intoxicating perfume reached him and fascinated him even where he stood.

'If I could only make one step across,' he thought, 'nothing could harm me if I only plucked that one flower, and nobody would know I had been over at all,' for the villagers looked with hatred and suspicion on anyone who was said to have crossed to the 'other side', so summing up courage he leapt lightly to the other side of the brook. Then the moon breaking from a cloud shone with unusual brilliance, and he saw, stretching before him, long reaches of the same strange blue flowers, each one lovelier than the last, till, not being able to make up his mind which one flower to take or whether to take several, he went on and on, and the moon shone very brightly and a strange unseen bird, somewhat like a nightingale, but louder and lovelier, sang, and his heart was filled with longing for he knew not what, and the moon shone and the nightingale sang. But on a sudden a black cloud covered the moon entirely, and all was black, utter darkness, and through the darkness he heard wolves howling and shrieking in the hideous ardour of the chase, and there passed before him a horrible procession of wolves (black wolves with red fiery eyes), and with them men that had the heads of wolves and wolves that had the heads of men, and above them flew owls (black owls with red fiery eyes) and bats and long serpentine black things, and last of all seated on an enormous black ram with hideous human face the wolf-keeper on whose face was eternal shadow; but they continued their horrid chase and passed him by, and when they had passed the moon shone out more beautiful than ever, and the strange nightingale sang again, and the strange intense blue flowers were in long reaches in front to the right and to the left. But one thing was there which had not been before; among the deep blue flowers walked one with long gleaming golden hair, and she turned once round and her eyes were of the same colour as the strange blue flowers, and she walked on and Gabriel could not choose but follow. But when a cloud passed over the moon he saw no beautiful woman but a wolf, so in utter terror he turned and fled, plucking one of the strange blue flowers on the way, and leapt again over the brook and ran home.

When he got home Gabriel could not resist showing his treasure to his mother, though he knew she would not appreciate it; but when she saw the strange blue flower, Mère Yvonne turned pale and said, 'Why child, where hast thou been? Sure it is the witch flower'; and so saying she snatched it from him and cast it into the corner, and immediately all its beauty and strange fragrance faded from it and it looked charred as though it had been burnt. So Gabriel sat down silently and rather sulkily, and having eaten no supper went up to bed, but he did got sleep but waited and waited till all was quiet within the house. Then he crept downstairs in his long white night-shirt and bare feet on the square cold stones and picked hurriedly up the charred and faded flower and put it in his warm bosom next his heart, and immediately the flower bloomed again lovelier than ever, and he fell into a deep sleep, but through his sleep he seemed to hear a soft low voice singing underneath his window in a strange language (in which the subtle sounds melted into one another), but he could distinguish no word except his own name.

When he went forth in the morning to serve Mass, he still kept the flower with him next his heart. Now when the priest began Mass and said '*Intrabo ad altare Dei*', then said Gabriel '*Qui nequiquam laetificavit juventutem meam*'. And the Abbé Félicien turned round on hearing this strange response, and he saw the boy's face deadly pale, his eyes fixed and his limbs rigid, and as the priest looked on him Gabriel fell fainting to the floor, so the sacristan had to carry him home and seek another acolyte for the Abbé Félicien.

Now when the Abbé Félicien came to see after him, Gabriel felt strangely reluctant to say anything about the blue flower and for the first time he deceived the priest.

In the afternoon as sunset drew nigh he felt better and Carmeille came to see him and begged him to go out with her into the fresh air. So they went out hand in hand, the dark haired, gazelle-eyed boy, and the fair wavy-haired girl, and something, he knew not what, led his steps (half knowingly and yet not so, for he could not but walk thither) to the brook, and they sat down together on the bank.

Gabriel thought at least he might tell his secret to Carmeille, so he took out the flower from his bosom and said, 'Look here, Carmeille, hast thou seen ever so lovely a flower as this?' but Carmeille turned pale and faint and said, 'Oh, Gabriel what is this flower? I but touched it and I felt something strange come over me. No, no, I don't like its perfume, no there's something not quite right about it, oh, dear Gabriel, do let me throw it away,' and before he had time to answer, she cast it from her, and again all its beauty and fragrance went from it and it looked charred as though it had been burnt. But suddenly where the flower had been thrown on this side of the brook, there appeared a wolf, which stood and looked at the children.

Carmeille said, 'What shall we do?' and clung to Gabriel, but the wolf looked at them very steadfastly and Gabriel recognised in the eyes of the wolf the strange deep intense blue eyes of the wolf-woman he had seen on the 'other side', so he said, 'Stay here, dear Carmeille, see she is looking gently at us and will not hurt us.'

'But it is a wolf,' said Carmeille, and quivered all over with fear, but again Gabriel said languidly, 'She will not hurt us.' Then Carmeille seized Gabriel's hand in an agony of terror and dragged him along with her till they reached the village, where she gave the alarm and all the lads of the village gathered together. They had never seen a wolf on this side of the brook, so they excited themselves greatly and arranged a grand wolf-hunt for the morrow, but Gabriel sat silently apart and said no word.

That night Gabriel could not sleep at all nor could he bring himself to say his prayers; but he sat in his little room by the window with his shirt open at the throat and the strange blue flower at his heart and again this night he heard a voice singing beneath his window in the same soft, subtle, liquid language as before –

> Ma zála liral va jé
> Cwamûlo zhajéla je
> Cárma urádi el javé
> Járma, symai, – carmé –
> Zhála javály thra je
> Al vú al vlaûle va azré
> Safralje vairálje va já?
> Cárma serâja
> Lâja lâja
> Luzhà!

and as he looked he could see the silvern shadows slide on the glimmering light of golden hair, and the strange eyes gleaming dark blue through the night and it seemed to him that he could not but follow; so he walked half clad and bare foot as he was with eyes fixed as in a dream silently down the stairs and out into the night.

And ever and again she turned to look on him with her strange blue eyes full of tenderness and passion and sadness beyond the sadness of things human – and as he foreknew, his steps led him to the brink of the brook. Then she, taking his hand, familiarly said, 'Won't you help me over, Gabriel?'

Then it seemed to him as though he had known her all his life – so he went with her to the 'other side' but he saw no-one by him; and looking again, beside him there were two wolves. In a frenzy of terror, he (who had never thought to kill any living thing before) seized a log of wood lying by and smote one of the wolves on the head.

Immediately he saw the wolf-woman again at his side with blood streaming from her forehead, staining her wonderful golden hair, and with eyes looking at him with infinite reproach, she said – 'Who did this?'

Then she whispered a few words to the other wolf, which leapt over the brook and made its way towards the village, and turning again towards him she said, 'Oh Gabriel, how could you strike me, who would have loved you so long and so well.' Then it seemed to him again as though he had known her all his life but he felt dazed and said nothing – but she gathered a dark green strangely shaped leaf and holding it to her forehead, she said – 'Gabriel, kiss the place all will be well again.' So he kissed as she had bidden him and he felt the salt taste of blood in his mouth and then he knew no more.

Again he saw the wolf-keeper with his horrible troupe around him, but this time not engaged in the chase but sitting in strange conclave in a circle and the black owls sat in the trees and the black bats hung downwards from the branches. Gabriel stood alone in the middle with a hundred wicked eyes fixed on him. They seemed to deliberate about what should be done with him, speaking in that same strange tongue which he had heard in the songs beneath his window. Suddenly he felt a hand pressing in his and saw the mysterious wolf-woman by his side. Then began what seemed a kind of incantation where human or half human creatures seemed to howl, and beasts to speak with human speech but in the unknown tongue. Then the wolf-keeper whose face was ever veiled in shadow spake some words in a voice that seemed to come from afar off, but all he could distinguish was his own name Gabriel and her name Lilith. Then he felt arms enlacing him.

Gabriel awoke – in his own room – so it was a dream after all – but what a dreadful dream. Yes, but was it his own room? Of course there was his coat hanging over the chair – yes but – the Crucifix – where was the Crucifix and the benetier and the con- secrated palm branch and the antique image of Our Lady *perpetuae salutis*, with the little ever-burning lamp before it, before which he placed every day the flowers he had gathered, yet had not dared to place the blue flower.

Every morning he lifted his still dream-laden eyes to it and said *Ave Maria* and made the sign of the cross, which bringeth peace to the soul – but how horrible, how maddening, it was not there, not at all. No surely he could not be awake, at least not *quite* awake, he would make the benedictive sign and he would be freed from this fearful illusion – yes but the sign, he would make the sign – oh, but what was the sign? Had he forgotten? Or was his arm paralysed? No he could not move. Then he had forgotten – and the prayer – he must remember that. *A – vae – nunc – mortis – fructus.* No surely it did not run thus – but something like it surely – yes, he was awake, he could move at any rate – he would reassure himself – he would get up – he would see the grey old church with the exquisitely pointed gables bathed in the light of dawn, and presently the deep solemn bell would toll and he would run down and don his red cassock and lace-worked cotta and light the tall candles on the altar and wait reverently to vest the good and gracious Abbé Félicien, kissing each vestment as he lifted it with reverent hands.

But surely this was not the light of dawn; it was like sunset! He leapt from his small white bed, and a vague terror came over him, he trembled and had to hold on to the chair before he reached the window. No, the solemn spires of the grey church were not to be seen – he was in the depths of the forest, but in a part he had never seen before – but surely he had explored every part, it must be the 'other side'. To terror succeeded a languor and lassitude not without charm – passivity, acquiescence, indulgence – he felt, as it were, the strong caress of another will flowing over him like water and clothing him with invisible hands in an impalpable garment; so he dressed himself almost mechanically and walked downstairs, the same stairs it seemed to him down which it was his wont to run and spring. The broad square stones seemed singularly beautiful and iridescent with many strange colours – how was it he had never noticed this before – but he was gradually losing the power of wondering – he entered the room below – the wonted coffee and bread-rolls were on the table.

'Why Gabriel, how late you are today.' The voice was very sweet but the intonation strange – and there sat Lilith, the mysterious wolf-woman, her glittering gold hair tied in a loose knot; an embroidery whereon she was tracing strange serpentine patterns, lay over the lap of her maize-coloured garment – and she looked at Gabriel steadfastly with her wonderful dark blue eyes and said, 'Why, Gabriel, you are late today,' and Gabriel answered, 'I was tired yesterday, give me some coffee.'

A dream within a dream – yes, he had known her all his life, and they dwelt together; had they not always done so? And she would take him through the glades of the forest and gather for him flowers, such as he had never seen before, and tell him stories in her strange, low deep voice, which seemed ever to be accompanied by the faint vibration of strings, looking at him fixedly the while with her marvellous blue eyes.

35

Little by little the flame of vitality which burned within him seemed to grow fainter and fainter, and his lithe lissom limbs waxed languorous and luxurious – yet was he ever filled with a languid content and a will not his own perpetually overshadowed him.

One day in their wanderings he saw a strange dark blue flower like unto the eyes of Lilith, and a sudden half remembrance flashed through his mind.

'What is this blue flower?' he said, and Lilith shuddered and said nothing; but as they went a little further there was a brook – *the* brook he thought, and felt his fetters falling off him, and he prepared to spring over the brook; but Lilith seized him by the arm and held him back with all her strength, and trembling all over she said, 'Promise me Gabriel that you will not cross over.'

But he said, 'Tell me what is this blue flower, and why you will not tell me?'

And she said, 'Look Gabriel at the brook.' And he looked and saw that though it was just like the brook of separation it was not the same, the waters did not flow.

As Gabriel looked steadfastly into the still waters it seemed to him as though he saw voices – some impression of the Vespers for the Dead. '*Hei mihi quia incolatus sum*', and again '*De profundis clamavi ad te*' – oh, that veil, that overshadowing veil! Why could he not hear properly and see, and why did he only remember as one looking through a threefold semi-transparent curtain. Yes they were praying for him – but who were they? He heard again the voice of Lilith in whispered anguish, 'Come away!'

Then he said, this time in monotone, 'What is this blue flower, and what is its use?'

And the low thrilling voice answered, 'it is called "lûli uzhûri", two drops pressed upon the face of the sleeper and he will *sleep*.'

He was as a child in her hand and suffered himself to be led from thence, nevertheless he plucked listlessly one of the blue flowers, holding it downwards in his hand. What did she mean? Would the sleeper wake? Would the blue flower leave any stain? Could that stain be wiped off?

But as he lay asleep at early dawn he heard voices from afar off praying for him – the Abbé Félicien, Carmeille, his mother too, then some familiar words struck his ear: '*Libera mea porta inferi.*' Mass was being said for the repose of his soul, he knew this. No, he could not stay, he would leap over the brook, he knew the way – he had forgotten that the brook did not flow. Ah, but Lilith would know – what should he do? The blue flower – there it lay close by his bedside – he understood now; so he crept very silently to where Lilith lay asleep, her long hair glistening gold, shining like a glory round about her. He pressed two drops on her forehead, she sighed once, and a shade of preternatural anguish passed over her beautiful face. He fled – terror, remorse, and hope tearing his soul and making fleet his feet. He came to the brook – he did not see that the water did not flow – of course it was the brook for separation; one bound, he should be with things human again. He leapt over and –

A change had come over him – what was it? He could not tell – did he walk on all fours? Yes surely. He looked into the brook, whose still waters were fixed as a mirror, and there, horror, he beheld himself; or was it himself? His head and face, yes; but his body transformed to that of a wolf. Even as he looked he heard a sound of hideous mocking laughter behind him. He turned round – there, in a gleam of red lurid light, he saw one whose body was human, but whose head was that of a wolf, with eyes of infinite malice; and, while this hideous being laughed with a loud human laugh, he, essaying to speak, could only utter the prolonged howl of a wolf.

But we will transfer our thoughts from the alien things on the 'other side' to the simple human village where Gabriel used to dwell. Mère Yvonne was not much surprised when Gabriel did not turn up to breakfast – he often did not, so absent-minded was he; this time she said, 'I suppose he has gone with the others to the wolf-hunt.' Not that Gabriel was given to hunting, but, as she sagely said, 'there was no knowing what he might do next.' The boys said, 'Of course that muff Gabriel is skulking and hiding himself, he's afraid to join the wolf-hunt; why, he wouldn't even kill a cat,' for their one notion of excellence was slaughter – so the greater the game the greater the glory. They were chiefly now confined to cats and sparrows, but they all hoped in after time to become generals of armies.

Yet these children had been taught all their life through with the gentle words of Christ – but alas, nearly all the seed falls by the wayside, where it could not bear flower or fruit; how little these know the suffering and bitter anguish or realise the full meaning of the words to those of whom it is written, 'Some fell among thorns.'

The wolf hunt was so far a success that they did actually see a wolf, but not a success, as they did not kill it before it leapt over the brook to the 'other side', where, of course, they were afraid to pursue it. No emotion is more inrooted and intense in the minds of common people than hatred and fear of anything 'strange'.

Days passed by but Gabriel was nowhere seen – and Mère Yvonne began to see clearly at last how deeply she loved her only son, who was so unlike her that she had thought herself an object of pity to other mothers – the goose and the swan's egg. People searched and pretended to search, they even went to the length of dragging the ponds, which the boys thought very amusing, as it enabled them to kill a great number of water rats, and Carmeille sat in a corner and cried all day long. Mère Pinquèle also sat in a corner and chuckled and said that she had always said Gabriel would come to no good. The Abbé Félicien looked pale and anxious, but said very little, save to God and those that dwelt with God.

At last, as Gabriel was not there, they supposed he must be no-where – that is *dead* (their knowledge of other localities being so limited, that it did not even occur to them to suppose he might be living elsewhere than in the village). So it was agreed that an empty catafalque should be put up in the church with tall candles round it, and Mère Yvonne said all the prayers that were in her prayer book, beginning at the beginning and ending at the end, regardless of their appropriateness – not even omitting the instructions of the rubrics. And Carmeille sat in the corner of the little side chapel and cried, and cried. And the Abbé Félicien caused the boys to sing the Vespers for the Dead (this did not amuse them so much as dragging the pond), and on the following morning, in the silence of early dawn, said the Dirge and the Requiem – *and this Gabriel heard.*

Then the Abbé Félicien received a message to bring the Holy Viaticum to one sick. So they set forth in solemn procession with great torches, and their way lay along the brook of separation.

Essaying to speak he could only utter the prolonged howl of a wolf – the most fearful of all bestial sounds. He howled and howled again – perhaps Lilith would hear him! Perhaps she could rescue him? Then he remembered the blue flower – the beginning and end of all his woe. His cries aroused all the denizens of the forest – the wolves, the wolf-men, and the men-wolves. He fled before them in an agony of terror – behind him, seated on the black ram with human face, was the wolf-keeper, whose face was veiled in eternal shadow. Only once he turned to look behind – for among the shrieks and howls of bestial chase he heard one thrilling voice moan with pain. And there among them he beheld Lilith, her body too was that of a wolf, almost hidden in the masses of her glittering golden hair, on her forehead was a stain of blue, like in colour to her mysterious eyes, now veiled with tears she could not shed.

The way of the Most Holy Viaticum lay along the brook of separation. They heard the fearful howlings afar off, the torch bearers turned pale and trembled – but the Abbé Félicien, holding aloft the Ciborium, said 'They cannot harm us.'

Suddenly the whole horrid chase came in sight. Gabriel sprang over the brook, the Abbé Félicien held the most Blessed Sacrament before him, and his shape was restored to him and he fell down prostrate in adoration. But the Abbé Félicien still held aloft the Sacred Ciborium, and the people fell on their knees in the agony of fear, but the face of the priest seemed to shine with divine effulgence. Then the wolf-keeper held up in his hands the shape of something horrible and inconceivable – a monstrance to the Sacrament of Hell, and three times he raised it, in mockery of the blessed rite of Benediction. And on the third time streams of fire went forth from his fingers, and all the 'other side' of the forest took fire, and great darkness was over all.

All who were there and saw and heard it have kept the impress thereof for the rest of their lives – nor till in their death hour was the remembrance thereof absent from their minds. Shrieks, horrible beyond conception, were heard till nightfall – then the rain rained.

The 'other side' is harmless now – charred ashes only; but none dares to cross but Gabriel alone – for once a year for nine days a strange madness comes over him.

A TERRIBLE TALE

Gaston Leroux

Captain Michel had but one arm, which he found useful when he lit his pipe. He was an old sea dog whose acquaintance, with that of four other old salts, I made one evening on the open front of a café in the Vieille Darse, Toulon, where I was taking an appetiser. And in this way we fell into the habit of foregathering over a glass within a stone's throw of the rippling waves and the swinging dinghys, about the hour when the sun sinks behind Tamaris.

The four old marines were known as Zinzin, Dorat—Captain Dorat—Bagatelle, and Chanlieu—that old fellow Chanlieu. They had, of course, sailed every sea and met with a thousand adventures; and now that they were retired on their pensions, they spent their time telling each other terrible tales.

Captain Michel alone never indulged in any reminiscences. And as he seemed in no way surprised by anything he heard, his old comrades in the end grew exasperated with him.

'Look here, Captain Michel, hasn't anything out of the way ever happened to you?'

'Oh yes,' the captain made answer, taking his pipe from his mouth. 'Yes, something happened to me once—just once.'

'Well, let's have it.'

'No.'

'Why not?'

'Because it's too awful. You might not be able to stand it. I've often tried to tell the story but people have slipped away before I finished it.'

The four sea dogs vied with each other in the loudness of their guffaws, declaring that Captain Michel was trying to find some excuse, because in reality, nothing extraordinary had ever happened to him.

The old fellow stared at them a moment, and then suddenly accepting the situation, laid his pipe on the table. This unusual gesture was in itself startling!

'Messieurs, I'll tell you how I lost my arm,' he began.

'In those days—some twenty years ago—I owned a small villa, in the suburb of Le Mourillon, which had been left to me, for my family were long settled in these parts and I myself was born here.

'It suited me to take a little rest after a long voyage and before setting sail again. For that matter, I rather liked the place, and lived quite peaceably among sea-faring men and colonials who troubled me very little, and whom I rarely saw, occupied as they were as a rule in opium-smoking with their lady friends, or with other business which did not concern me. Of course there is no accounting for tastes, but as long as they didn't interfere with me, I was satisfied . . .

'It so happened that one night they did interfere with my habit of going to sleep. I was awakened with a start by an extraordinary uproar, the meaning of which I couldn't possibly make out. I had left my window open as usual. I listened in a state of bewilderment to a tremendous din, which was a cross between the rumbling of thunder and the roll of a drum, but such a drum! It was as though a couple of hundred drumsticks were being madly beaten, not on ordinary drum-skin, but on a wooden drum.

'The disturbance came from the villa opposite, which had been empty for some five years, and on which I had noticed, the previous evening, a board bearing the announcement: "To be sold."

'I let my gaze stray from the window of my bedroom, on the first floor, beyond the small garden in which the house stood, and my eye took in every door and window, even the doors and windows on the ground floor. They were still closed as I had seen them during the day; but I caught sight of gleams of light through the chinks in the shutters on the ground floor. Who and what were these people? How had they found their way into this solitary house at the far end of Le Mourillon? What sort of company was it that had obtained admission into this deserted dwelling, and why were they kicking up such a shindy?

'The extraordinary din, like the thunderous beating of a wooden drum, continued. It went on for another hour, and then as dawn was breaking, the front door opened, and there appeared in the doorway the most radiant creature that I have ever beheld. She was clad in a low-necked dress, and held with perfect grace a lamp whose beams fell over the shoulders of a goddess. I distinctly heard her say in the echoing night, while a kind and quiet smile flickered across her face:

'"Good-bye, dear friend, till next year."

'To whom was she speaking? It was impossible for me to tell for I could see no one standing beside her. She remained at the entrance holding the lamp for some minutes, until the garden gate opened by itself and closed by itself. Then the front door of the house was shut in its turn, and I saw nothing more.

'It seemed to me that I was either losing my head or was the sport of a dream, for I knew that it was out of the question for anyone to pass through the garden without my perceiving him.

'I was still planted at the window, incapable of the least movement or thought, when the door of the house opened a second time, and the same vision of beauty appeared still carrying a lamp and still alone.

'"Hush," she said, "Don't make a noise any of you. We mustn't disturb our neighbour opposite. I'll come with you."

'And silently and alone she crossed the garden and stopped at the gate on which the full rays of the lamp shone; so much so, indeed, that I clearly saw the knob of the gate turn of its own accord without any hand being placed upon it. And the gate opened once again by itself in the presence of this woman who, moreover, did not evince any surprise. Need I explain that from where I was posted, I could see both in front and behind the gate; in other words, that I saw it sideways?

'This "splendid apparition" made a charming movement of her head towards the empty darkness which the glare of the lamp made visible; then she smiled and said:

'"Well, good-bye until next year. My husband is very pleased. Not a single one of you failed to answer the call. Good-bye, messieurs."

'And I heard several voices in unison:

'"Good-bye, madame, good-bye, dear madame, until next year."

'And as the mysterious hostess was preparing to close the door herself, I heard a voice:

'"Oh, please, don't trouble."

'And the door was once more closed.

'The next moment the air was filled with a curious sound; it was like the chirping of a flock of birds, and it seemed as if this beautiful woman had opened the cage of a whole brood of house sparrows.

'She quietly walked back to the house. The lights on the ground floor were then out, but I noticed a glimmer in the windows of the first floor.

'When she reached the house she said:

'"Are you upstairs, Gérard?"

'I could not hear the answer, but the front door was again closed, and a few minutes later the light on the first floor went out.

'I was still standing at my window at eight o'clock in the morning, staring in blank amazement at the house and garden which had revealed such strange happenings in darkness, and which now in the full light of day assumed their familiar aspect. The garden was a waste, and the house itself seemed as desolate as it was the day before.

'So much so, indeed, that when I told my old charwoman who had just come, of the queer events which I had witnessed, she tapped my forehead with her dirty forefinger and muttered that I had smoked one pipe too many. Now I have never been a smoker of opium, and her answer gave me a good opportunity of sacking the old sloven whom I had for some time wanted to get rid of, and who came for a couple of hours each day to "clean up" the place for me. For that matter I did not need any one, as I was setting sail again next day.

'I barely had time to put my things together, make a few purchases, say farewell to my friends, and catch the train for Havre. I had fixed up an appointment with the Transatlantic company which would keep me away from Toulon for some eleven or twelve months.

'In due course I returned to Toulon, but though I had refrained from mentioning my adventure to a soul, I still continued to think of it. The vision of the lady of the lamp obsessed me wherever I went, and the last words which she uttered to her unseen friends still rang in my ears:

'"Well, good-bye until next year."

'And I never ceased to think of the meeting. I, too, was determined to be there and to discover, at whatever cost, the solution of a mystery which was intensely perplexing to a sensible man like myself, who did not believe in ghosts or phantom vessels.

'Unfortunately I was soon to learn that neither heaven nor hell were concerned in the terrible story.

'It was six o'clock in the evening when I set foot again in my house at Toulon; and it was two days before the anniversary of the wonderful night.

'The first thing that I did on going inside was to run up to my room and open the window. It was summer and broad daylight, and my eyes at once fell upon a lady of great beauty who was placidly walking about gathering flowers in the garden of the house opposite. At the noise made by the opening window she looked up.

'It was the lady of the lamp. I recognised her, and she seemed not less beautiful by day than by night. Her skin was as white as the teeth of an African, her eyes bluer than the waters at Tamaris, her hair as soft and fair as the finest flax.

'Why should I not make the confession? When I beheld this woman of whom I had been dreaming for a year, a strange feeling came over me. She was no illusion of a diseased imagination. She stood before me in the flesh; and every window of the house was open and flower-bedecked by her hands. There was nothing fantastic in all this.

'She caught sight of me and at once displayed some degree of annoyance. She walked a few steps farther in the centre path of the garden, and then shrugging her shoulders as though she were disconcerted said:

'"Let's go in, Gérard. I'm beginning to feel the coolness of the night."

'I let my gaze stray round the garden. I could perceive no one. To whom was she speaking? . . . Nobody there!

'Then was she mad? It scarcely seemed so.

'I watched her return to the house. She passed into it, the door was closed, and she at once shut the windows.

'I did not see or hear anything worth noticing that night. Next morning at ten o'clock I observed my neighbour leaving the garden attired as if for a walk. She locked the gate after her and set out in the direction of Toulon.

'I started off in my turn. Pointing to the fashionably dressed figure in front of me I asked the first tradesman whom I met if he knew the lady's name.

'"Why, of course. She's your neighbour. She is living with her husband at the Villa Makoko. They moved in about a year ago, just as you went away. They are regular boors. They never speak to anybody, unless it's absolutely necessary, but every one in Le Mourillon, as you know, goes his own way, and is never surprised at anything. The captain for one . . ."

'"What captain?"

'"Captain Gérard. It seems he is an ex-captain of marines. Well, no one ever sees him . . . Sometimes when food has to be delivered at the house, and the lady is not in, some person shouts out an order from behind the door to leave the stuff on the step, and waits until you are a good distance away before taking it in."

'You can imagine that I was growing more and more puzzled. I went to Toulon in order to ask the agent who let the villa a few questions about these people. He, likewise, had never seen the husband, but he told me that his name was Gérard Beauvisage.

'When I heard the name I uttered a cry: "Gérard Beauvisage! Why I know him!"

'I had an old friend of that name whom I had not seen for twenty-five years. He was an officer in the marines and had left Toulon for Tonkin about that period. How could I doubt that it was he? At all events, I had a straightforward reason for calling on him, that very evening, though he was expecting a visit from his friends, for it was the anniversary of the famous night. I made up my mind to renew my old friendship with him.

'When I got back to Le Mourillon I espied in front of me, in the sunk road leading to the Villa Makoko, the figure of my neighbour. I did not hesitate, but hastened to overtake her.

'"Have I the honour of speaking to Madame Beauvisage, the wife of Captain Gérard Beauvisage?" I asked with a bow.

'She coloured and tried to pass on without answering me.

'"Madame, I am your neighbour, Captain Michel Alban," I persisted.

'"Oh please forgive me, monsieur," she returned, "my husband has often spoken of you . . . Captain Michel Alban . . ."

'She seemed terribly ill at ease, and yet in her confusion, she was more beautiful than ever, if that were possible. In spite of her obvious desire to elude me I went on:

'"How comes it that Captain Beauvisage has returned to France without letting his old friend know? I shall be particularly obliged if you will tell Gérard that I'm coming to shake hands with him this very evening."

'And observing that she was hastening her steps, I bowed, but as I was speaking she turned round, betraying an agitation which was more and more difficult to comprehend.

'"Impossible to-night . . . I promise to tell Gérard of our meeting. That's the most I can do. Gérard doesn't wish to see anyone—anyone. He lives alone . . . We live alone . . . And we took the house because we were told that the next house was occupied only for a few days once or twice a year by someone who is never seen! . . ."

'And she added in a voice tinged with sadness:

'"You must forgive Gérard, monsieur. We do not receive anyone—anyone. Good day, monsieur."

'"Madame, the Captain and you receive friends occasionally," I returned with some impatience. "For instance, tonight you are expecting friends with whom you made an appointment a year ago."

'She flushed scarlet.

'"Oh, but that's an exceptional case . . . that's an absolutely exceptional case . . . They are our very particular friends."

'Having said which she made her escape, but at once stopped her retreat and turned back.

'"Whatever you do, don't call tonight", she entreated, and disappeared into the garden.

'I returned to my house and began to keep watch on my neighbours. They did not show themselves, and long before it was dark I saw the shutters being closed and lights gleaming through the openings, such as I had seen on that amazing night a year ago. But I did not hear the same extraordinary din like the thunderous beating of a wooden drum.

'At seven o'clock I began to dress for I called to mind the low-necked robe worn by the lady of the lamp. Madame Beauvisage's last words had but strengthened my determination. The captain was seeing some of his friends that evening; he dared not refuse me admission. After dressing it crossed my mind, before I went downstairs, to put my revolver in my pocket, but in the end I left it in its place, considering that to take it would be an act of stupidity.

'The stupidity lay in not taking it with me.

'On reaching the entrance to the Villa Makoko I turned the handle of the gate on the off chance—the handle which last year I had seen turn by itself. And to my intense surprise the door opened. Therefore my neighbours were expecting visitors. I walked up to the house and knocked at the door.

'"Come in!" a voice cried.

'I recognised Gérard's voice. I walked gaily into the house. I passed first through the hall, and then as the door of a small drawing-room stood open, and the room was lit up, I entered it.

'"Gérard it's me," I exclaimed, "your old pal Michel Alban."

'"Oh, really, so you made up your mind to come, my dear old Michel! I told my wife only just now that you would come and I should be glad to see you . . . But you are the only one, apart from our particular friends . . . Do you know, my dear Michel, you haven't altered much . . ."

'It would be impossible for me to describe my stupefaction. I heard Gérard, but I could not see him. His voice rang in my ears, but no one was near me, no one was in the drawing-room. The Voice went on:

'"Sit down, won't you? My wife will soon be here, for she will remember that she left me on the mantelpiece!"

'I looked up, and then discovered above me . . . above me resting on a high mantelpiece—a bust.

'It was this bust which had been speaking. It resembled Gérard. It was Gérard's body. It had been placed there as people are wont to place busts on mantelpieces. It was a bust like those carved by sculptors, that is to say, it was without arms.

'"I can't shake hands with you, my dear Michel," the voice went on, "for as you see I have no hands, but if you raise yourself on tiptoe you will be able to take me in your arms and place me on the table. My wife put me up here in a moment of temper, because she said I was in the way when she swept the room. She's a funny thing is my wife."

'And the bust burst out laughing.

'It seemed to me that I was the victim of an optical illusion as happens in those entertainments where you behold living heads and shoulders suspended in mid-air, the result of tricks with mirrors; but after setting down my friend on the table, as he requested, I had to admit that this head and body without arms or legs was indeed all that remained of the excellent officer whom I had known in days gone by. His body was resting on a small wheeled platform, such as are used by cripples without legs, but Gérard did not possess even the stumps of legs which can be seen in the case of most cripples. To think that my old friend was nothing but a bust!

'Small hooks took the place of arms, and language fails me to describe how, leaning for support on a hook here, or on another there, he set to work to hop, skip and jump and perform a hundred swift movements which shot him from the table to a chair, from a chair to the floor, and then suddenly made him appear on the table once more, where he indulged in the gayest chatter.

'Myself, I was in a state of consternation. I was rendered speechless. I watched this freak perform his antics and say with a chuckle which alarmed me:

'"I have greatly changed I daresay. You must admit, my dear Michel, that you hardly recognise me. You did quite right to call this evening. We shall see some sport. We have a few very special friends, and, you know, apart from them I don't care to meet anyone—merely as a matter of pride. We don't even keep a servant. Wait for me here. I must get into my smoking jacket."

'He went off, and almost at once the lady of the lamp appeared.

She wore the same low-necked dress of the year before. As soon as her eyes fell upon me, she seemed strangely perturbed, and said in a strained voice:

'"Oh, so you are here! You've made a mistake, Captain Michel. I gave your message to my husband, but I forbade you to call this evening. I may tell you that when he learnt that you were in this place, he asked me to invite you this evening, but I did no such thing because," she went on, ill at ease, "I had good reasons. We have certain very particular friends who are rather a worry—they are very fond of noise—uproar. You must have heard them last year," she added, giving me a look out of the corner of her eye. "Well, promise me to leave early."

'"I promise to leave early, madame," I returned, and yet a vague misgiving took possession of me at this conversation the meaning of which I was far from understanding. "I promise you faithfully, but can you tell me how it is that I find my old friend in such a state? What terrible accident happened to him?"

'"None at all, monsieur, none."

'"What do you mean, 'none at all'? Don't you know anything about the accident which deprived him of arms and legs. Yet he must have met with it since your marriage."

'"No, monsieur, no. I married the captain as he is now . . . But excuse me, our guests will be here presently, and I must help my husband to put on his smoking jacket."

'She left me to myself, dazed by the one stupefying thought: "She married the captain as he is now!" and almost at once I heard sounds in the hall, the curious sounds which had accompanied the lady of the lamp to the garden gate and baffled me last year. This noise was followed by the appearance, on their wheeled platforms, of four cripples without arms or legs who stared at me in wonder. They were all attired in perfectly-fitting evening dress with snow-white shirt fronts.

'One wore gold-rimmed pince-nez, another, an old man, spectacles, the third a single eye-glass, and the fourth was content to gaze at me out of his own proud, shrewd eyes with an expression of boredom. All four, however, saluted me with their little hooks, and asked after Captain Beauvisage. I told them that he was dressing, and Madame Beauvisage was quite well. When I took the liberty of speaking of Madame Beauvisage, I caught an exchange of glances between them which seemed to embody a certain raillery.

'"Haw, haw, I presume you are a great friend of our good old captain," drawled the cripple with the monocle.

'The others smiled with a look which was by no means pleasant, and then they all started to talk in the same breath:

'"Sorry, sorry, monsieur . . . We are quite naturally surprised to meet you at the house of the good old captain, who swore on his wedding day to shut himself up in the country with his wife, and not to receive anyone—anyone but his very special friends, you understand. When one is so thoroughly a cripple as the captain consented to be, and is married to such a beautiful woman, it is quite natural—quite natural. But, after all, if in the course of his life he met a man of honour who does not happen to be a cripple, we're glad of it . . . We congratulate you."

'And they repeated: "We're glad of it . . . We congratulate you."

'Lord how odd they were, these dwarfs! I watched them and held my peace. Others arrived in twos and threes and so on. And they all contemplated me with a look of surprise or uneasiness or irony. For my part I was rendered speechless by the spectacle of so many cripples without arms or legs; for after all I was beginning to see through most of the extraordinary happenings which had so greatly stirred my mind; and though the cripples, by their presence, explained many things, the presence of the cripples still required explanation, as also did the monstrous union of that splendid woman with that awful shred of humanity.

'True, I realised now that these little ambulating trunks were bound to pass unperceived by me in the narrow garden path lined with verbena, and the road running between two low hedges; and, truth to tell, when at the time I said to myself that it was impossible to avoid seeing any person going down those paths, I had in mind persons who would be standing upright on their two legs.

'The handle of the garden gate itself no longer puzzled me, and in my mind's eye I saw the invisible hook which had turned it.

'The peculiar noise which I heard was but the creaking made by the small badly oiled wheels of these cars for freaks. Finally, the extraordinary sound like the thunderous beating of a wooden drum, was obviously caused by the many cars and hooks striking the floor when, after an excellent dinner, our friends the cripples indulged in a dance.

'Yes all this was capable of explanation but I was conscious as I caught a curious eager gleam in their eyes, and heard the peculiar sound of their nippers, that something terrible still remained to be cleared up, and that all else which had surprised me was of no account.

'Meanwhile Madame Beauvisage promptly appeared, accompanied by her husband. They were greeted with shouts of delight. The little hooks "applauded" them with an infernal din. I was deafened by it. Then I was introduced. Cripples were all over the place: on the tables, chairs, stools, on stands usually occupied by vases, on the sideboard. One of them sat on the shelf of a dresser like a Buddha in his recess. And each one politely held out his hook to me. They seemed for the most part people of good position, with titles and names indicating their relationship to aristocratic families, but I learned afterwards that these were false names given to me for reasons which will be obvious. Lord Wilmer certainly maintained the best front of them all, with his fine golden beard and no less fine moustache which he continually stroked with his hook. He did not leap from chair to table like the others, nor did he have the air of a huge bat taking wing from wall to wall.

'"We are only waiting for the doctor," said the mistress of the house, who every now and then gave me a look of obvious gloom, but quickly resumed her smile for her guests.

'The doctor arrived. He was a cripple but he possessed both arms.

'He offered one of them to Madame Beauvisage and led her to the dining-room. I mean that she touched his arm with the tips of her fingers.

'Covers were laid in the room with the closed shutters. The table, which was laden with flowers and *hors d'œuvre*, was illuminated by a large candelabrum. There was no fruit. The dozen cripples at once leapt upon their chairs and began to pick greedily from the dishes with their hooks. It was not a pleasant sight, and I marvelled at the voracity with which these trunks of men, who seemed just before so well-mannered, devoured their food.

'And then suddenly they quietened down; their hooks kept still, and it seemed to me that they lapsed into what is usually described as a "painful silence."

'Every eye was turned on Madame Beauvisage, whose husband sat by her side, and I noticed that she buried her face in her napkin, looking very uncomfortable. Then my friend Gérard, clapping one hook against the other with a flourish, said:

'"Well, my dear old friends, it can't be helped. One doesn't meet the luck of last year every day. But don't distress yourselves. With the exercise of a little imagination we shall succeed in being as merry as we were then . . ."

'And turning to me as he lifted the small handle of the glass which stood on the table before him:

'"Your health my dear Michel. To us all!"

'And each man raised his glass by its handle with the end of his hook. The glasses swung over the table in the quaintest fashion.

'My host went on:

'"You don't seem to be equal to the occasion, my dear Michel. I have known you in merrier mood, more up to the mark. Is it because we are 'like this' that you are so gloomy? What do you expect? We are what we are. But let us have some amusement. We are met together here, all of us very special friends, to celebrate the time when we became 'like this.' Is that not true my friends of the *Daphné?* . . .''

'Then my old comrade,' Captain Michel went on to explain, heaving a deep sigh, 'told us how the *Daphné*, which sailed between France and the Far East, was wrecked; how the crew escaped in the boats, and how these miserable people took refuge on a chance raft.

'Miss Madge, a beautiful young girl who lost her parents in the catastrophe, was also picked up by the raft. Some thirteen persons in all were on it, and at the end of three days the victuals were consumed, and at the end of a week the survivors were dying of hunger. It was then that, as the old song says, they agreed to draw lots as to "which should be eaten."

'Messieurs,' added Captain Michel, in a serious voice, 'such things have happened more often perhaps than they have been talked about, for the great blue waters close over these peculiar feats of digestion.

'They were on the point, therefore, of drawing lots on the raft when the doctor's voice was heard: "Mesdames and Messieurs," said the doctor, "You have lost all your belongings in the wreck of the ship, but I have saved my case of instruments and my forceps for arresting haemorrhage. This is my suggestion: There is no object in any one of us running the risk of being eaten as a whole. Let us, to begin with, draw lots of an arm or leg at will, and we will then see tomorrow what the day brings forth, and perhaps a sail may appear on the horizon."'

At this point in Captain Michel's story the four old salts, who up to this had not interrupted, cried:

'Well done!'

'What do you mean "well done"?' asked Captain Michel with a frown.

'Yes, "well done!" Your story is a good joke. These people were ready to lose an arm or leg in turn . . . That's a good joke, but there's nothing frightful about it.'

'So you really find it a good joke!' growled the Captain, bristling with annoyance. 'Well, I swear that if you had been seated among all those cripples whose eyes were bulging like live coal, and heard the story, you wouldn't have found it such a good joke . . . And if you had noticed how restless they were in their chairs! And how vigorously they clasped hooks across the table with an obvious delight which I couldn't make out, but which was none the less frightful for all that.'

'No, no,' broke in Chanlieu once more—that old fellow Chanlieu—'your story is not in the least frightful. It is funny simply because it is logical. Would you like me to tell you the end of the story? You shall say whether I am right or not. The people on the raft drew lots. The lot fell to Miss Madge who was to lose one of her beautiful limbs. Your friend the captain, who is a gentleman, offered his own instead, and he had his four limbs amputated so that Miss Madge should remain unscathed.'

'Yes, old man, you've got it. That is so,' exclaimed Captain Michel who felt a longing to break the heads of these imbeciles who treated his story as a good joke. 'Yes, and what's more, when it was a question of cutting off Miss Madge's limbs after the survivors, except the young lady and the doctor—who had been left with both arms because they were wanted—had lost all their limbs, Captain Beauvisage had the pluck to have the poor stumps left from the first operation, cut off on a level with his body.'

'And the young lady could do no other than offer the Captain her hand which he had so heroically saved,' interposed Zinzin.

'Why, of course,' growled the Captain in his beard. 'And you consider it a good joke!'

'Did they eat all those limbs quite raw?' enquired that ass of a Bagatelle.

Captain Michel struck the table such a resounding blow that the glasses danced like rubber balls.

'That'll do, shut up,' he exclaimed. 'All that I've told you is nothing. Now comes the frightful part of it.'

The four friends looked at each other smiling, and Captain Michel grew pale, whereupon seeing that they had carried matters too far they hung their heads.

'Yes, the frightful part of it,' went on Michel with his gloomiest air, 'was that these people who were only rescued a month later by a Chinese sailing vessel which landed them somewhere on the Yang-Tse-Kiang where they separated—the frightful part of it was that these people retained a taste for human flesh, and when they returned to Europe arranged to meet together once a year to renew as far as possible the abominable banquet. Well, messieurs, it did not take me long to find that out! First of all there was the scarcely enthusiastic reception accorded to certain dishes, which Madame Beauvisage herself brought to the table. Though she ventured to claim, but with no great assurance, that they were pretty nearly the same thing, the guests were of one mind in abstaining from congratulating her. Only certain slices of tunny-fish were received with any sort of favour, because they were, to use the doctor's terrible expression, "well cut," and, "if the flavour was not entirely satisfactory at all events the eye was deceived." But the cripple with the spectacles met with general approval when he declared that "it was not equal to the plumber."

'When I heard those words I felt my blood run cold,' growled Captain Michel huskily, 'for I remembered that about this time the year before a plumber had fallen from a roof near the Arsenal and was killed, and his body was picked up minus an arm.

'Then . . . O then . . . I could not help thinking of the part which my beautiful neighbour must, of necessity, have played in this horrible, culinary drama. I turned my eyes to her and I noticed that she had put on her gloves again, gloves which covered her arms to the shoulder, and also hastily thrown a wrap over her shoulders which wholly concealed them. The guest on my right, who was the doctor, and, as I have said, was the only man among the cripples with both arms intact, had also put on his gloves.

'Instead of bothering my head in vain to discover the reason of this fresh eccentricity, I should have done better to follow the advice which Madame Beauvisage gave me at the beginning of this infernal party, namely, to leave the place early—advice which she did not repeat.'

'After showing an interest in me during the first part of this amazing feast in which I seemed to discern—I don't know why—a sort of pity, Madame Beauvisage now avoided looking at me and took a part which greatly grieved me in the most frightful conversation which I have ever heard. These little people with a vigorous clatter of nippers and clinking of glasses indulged in bitter recriminations or warm congratulations with regard to their peculiar appetite.

'To my horror Lord Wilmer who until then had been most correct, nearly 'came to hooks' with the cripple with the monocle, because the latter had once on the raft complained of the former being tough, and the mistress of the house had the greatest difficulty in putting things in their true light by retorting to the monocled bust, who was obviously at the time of the shipwreck a good-looking stripling, that neither was it particularly agreeable to have to put up with "an animal that was too young."'

'That's also funny,' the old salt Dorat could not help interjecting.

It looked as if Captain Michel would fly at his throat, particularly as the three other mariners seemed to be shaking with inward joy and gave vent to queer little clucks. It was as much as the Captain could do to control himself. After puffing like a seal he turned to the foolhardy Dorat:

'Monsieur you have two arms still, and I have no wish for you to lose one of them, as I did on that particular night, to make you see the frightful part of the story. The cripples had drunk a great deal. Some of them jumped on the table round me, and were gazing at my arms in a very embarrassing manner and I ended by hiding them from sight as far as possible by thrusting my hands deep into my pockets.

'I realised then, and it was a startling thought, why Madame Beauvisage and the doctor, the two persons who still had arms and hands, did not show them. I grasped the meaning of the sudden ferocity which blazed in the eyes of some of them. And at that very moment, as luck would have it, I wanted to use my pocket handkerchief, and instinctively I made a movement which revealed the whiteness of my skin under my sleeve, and three terrible hooks swooped down at once on my wrist and entered my flesh. I uttered a fearful shriek.'

'That'll do, Captain, that'll do,' I exclaimed, interrupting Captain Michel's story. 'You were quite right. I'm off. I can't stand any more.'

'Stay, monsieur,' said the Captain in a peremptory tone. 'Stay, monsieur, for I shall soon finish this frightful story which has made four imbeciles laugh. When a man has Phocean blood in his veins,' he added with an accent of unspeakable contempt turning to the four ancient mariners who were obviously choking in their efforts to keep back their laughter, 'when a man has Phocean blood in his veins, he can't get over it.

'And when a man lives in Marseilles he is doomed never to believe in anything. So it is for you, for you alone, monsieur, that I am telling this story, and, be assured, I will pass over the most loathsome details, knowing as I do how much the mind of a gentleman can bear. The tragedy of my martyrdom proceeded so quickly that I can call to mind only their inhuman cries, the protests of some and the rush of others while Madame Beauvisage stood up and murmured:

'"Be careful not to hurt him!"

'I tried to leap to my feet, but by this time a posse of mad cripples was round me who tripped me up and I crashed to the floor. And I felt their awful hooks hold my flesh captive just as the meat in a butcher's shop is held captive on its hooks.

'Yes, monsieur, I will spare you the details. I pledged you my word; all the more so as I couldn't give them to you, for I did not see the operation. The doctor clapped a plug of cotton wool steeped in chloroform on my mouth by way of a gag.

'When I came to myself I was in the kitchen, and I had lost an arm. The cripples were all around me. They had ceased their wrangling. They seemed to be united in the most touching harmony; in reality they were in a state of dazed intoxication which caused them to sway their heads like children who feel the need to go and lie down after eating their fill, and I had not a doubt but that they were beginning, alas! to digest me . . . I was stretched at full length on the floor, securely bound, and deprived of all power of movement, but I could both see and hear them. My old comrade, Gérard Beauvisage, had tears of joy in his eyes as he exclaimed:

'"I should never have thought you would be so tender!"

'Madame Beauvisage was not present, but she, too, must have taken part in the feast, for I heard someone ask Gérard how "she liked her share."

'Yes, monsieur, I have finished my story. I have finished my story. Those loathsome cripples having satisfied their weakness, must have at last realised the full extent of their iniquity. They made themselves scarce, and Madame Beauvisage, of course, escaped with them. They left the doors wide open but no one came to set me free until four days afterwards, when I was pretty well dead with hunger . . .

'Those miserable wretches had not even left the bone behind!'

American Zombie

Dr Gordon Leigh Bromley

Paris in 1936 was pleasant when I drove from Le Bourget Airport into the city one spring morning. I had boarded the first flight out of London on a rapid visit, and intended to cover a number of disparate quests. A writer in the Parisian newspaper *Le Temps* had printed certain views on modern commercial art; and I wanted to ask him further questions. Other interviews ended, I rang up the office, enquired for M. Henri Champley, and mentioned I had a note from their London correspondent, Robert L. Cru. He was away, they said, at the *Agence Havas*, but would I come now, as he was due back soon?

When I entered the office I had not the slightest intention of making any mention of my own interest in magic; but a chance remark was made by Madame Tabouis – who happened to call at the same time – concerning the exploits of Madame Alexandra David-Neel, whom I had met in Benares many years back, before she went to Tibet. I found M. Champley deeply interested in a book he had just finished correcting; and he was profoundly involved in Negro culture in its every aspect. He had already published a book named, I think, *Route Shanghai*; and this new work was to be *Femme Blanc et L'Homme Noir*, or some similar title – it had not been finally settled. Recently I had reviewed W. B. Seabrook's volumes, *Magic Island* and *Jungle Ways*; and when my ordinary query was done and out of the way, our conversation became directed to experiences of magic. Despite his wide travels, M. Champley did not claim to any close experience of the occult side of the world, even though he had been through the Orient. Probably he kept too much to the well-trodden tracks of the very affluent folk. He had been through the Netherlands, East Indies, too; Java, and of course, Bali, and I imagine also in Sumatra; but even there he had sought no contact with the hidden world. The ordinary underworld of the civilised white, yes; that was, indeed, one of his interests as a good newspaperman and a student of world affairs! He was frankly alarmed at the intercourse of white men with coloured women, and – what seemed more serious to him – that of white women and the coloured men. He could understand, he said, the German revulsion against this biological revolution. I referred to the French colonies, and what I had myself seen. All this he admitted – from Morocco to Indo-China. And then he mentioned Haiti – and zombies; and then Seabrook's account came to mind.

Henri Champley then calmly remarked: 'But yes, I have myself seen a zombie! And not in Haiti, but in New York! And a white woman!'

Even among students of magic, the phenomenon of the zombie is rarely mentioned. The zombie, the vampire, the ghoul, and the modern versions of the incubi and the succubi – they are not pleasant. One needs a stout heart and some knowledge to examine them coolly. Among the Bataks in Sumatra I had found the zombie and though I was on the best occasion not alone, her owner was too near the district for my liking.

I asked M. Champley to tell me about this American zombie. He paused for several silent moments before replying. It seemed he had tried to forget an unpleasant experience; and it was now hard to recall sufficient facts of the event.

Finally he began, slowly: 'You remember what Madame David-Neel tells about her experiences in Tibet?'

I nodded assent, having read her books carefully.

'There was a man – several men – who became rapid travellers, helped through being in a half-hypnotic state. Well, that seems to me to be a sort of approach to the zombie; but now it endures longer. The creature may otherwise be dead to this world.'

My own experience concurred with that observation. There are zombies of many degrees and several kinds. Even in the streets of London the living dead may at intervals be seen, moving about on some task at the will of their masters. But I was interested to hear of this American zombie.

'I was staying in New York City,' continued M. Champley, 'and naturally I turned to Harlem, the principal Negro district, for my own studies in Negro culture!'

He had attended a sort of secret society meeting, held in a cellar in Lennox Avenue, after the ordinary Harlem 'joints' had closed down. There the Negroes were discussing political aspects of their future. One of them, whom he called Mr Joshua, walked downtown as far as Central Park. In the early morning sunshine many topics were broached. They discussed the attractions between white people and coloured people. Mr Joshua became more mysterious when the subject of 'fascination' came up, said M. Champley.

'Joshua hinted that the Negroes still possessed some of the ancient secrets of magic – those known in the Congo, in Guinea, centuries ago. These traditional methods of magic, he asserted, the Chinese or Japanese knew nothing about. As to that, I do not myself know if that is correct.

'Then he asked me, if I knew what is a *guédé*. The name was utterly strange to me. Then he said, it is a zombie. At once I recognised the term, from Seabrook's book, and said so; but I did not know more than the slight description,

there printed, could tell me. That was not much and I told
Joshua that it was off my beat!

' "Well," he said very proudly, as if the Negro magician
must be very great in order to have gained this power – and
perhaps he is, too! – "you can think it is a dead body,
brought to life once more, before all of the life has departed.
Or you may say it is perhaps an ordinary human, whose
will has been completely subdued. His own intelligence is
suppressed; it will never rise again. He understands sufficient to hear and to obey, but never rises into personal
consciousness again!"

' "This is the same as hypnotism?" I asked.

' "But no! Not the same," said my friend Joshua. "It is a
slavery of the soul. And I have seen it!" '

Then I put a question: 'What precisely *is* the difference
between a process of hypnotism – such as the system they
used years ago at the Salpêtriere for medical purposes or
psychological research – and this occult process of fascination, which has produced the zombie? What is the difference between ordinary hypnotism – and the allied but not
identical method of mesmerism?'

Champley confessed himself unable to define them. I had
seen both hypnotism and mesmerism practised; and I felt
sure there was a considerable difference. Without going into
detail here, I felt that one process was operated directly
through the mind, the other chiefly through the body. Or
putting it otherwise, you could mesmerise an animal – a cat,
or a hen – but it was not possible to hypnotise a being which
had not got a conscious mind to be hypnotised. I explained,
as well as I could, some of these points.

'But,' I asked, 'how is the zombie produced? Is it an
obsession?'

Again Champley admitted his ignorance. He did not
know; he had not been told. He told us more about his New
York adventure.

'Mr Joshua told me of a mysterious old Negro, whom he
knew personally, who had claimed the power to produce

and control the zombies. He had first shown this American zombie to Joshua, as an example, for him not to fear the power of the whites. For here was a white woman or what had once been a white woman, now one of the living dead.

'In a bedroom, on a higher floor of a Harlem rooming-house, that was actually over the restaurant cellar where I had attended the Negro meeting, was a locked room. In this room was the hiding-place of the American zombie. The old Negro unlocked the door silently. He approached the bed, which bore a silent form, covered by a sort of cheap table-cloth. He drew back this cloth, revealing a deathly waxen face of a woman of perhaps thirty, dark-haired. He took the cover completely off. Her arms rested by her sides, and her torso and limbs glowed with a peculiar waxen pallor. There was not a spot of colour on her, no other hair, and the nipples were like white roots of some plant.

'The old Negro stood back, his arms folded, as he muttered some ancient Congo exhortation; and presently the woman stood up, folded the cloth around her, and began to move about, performing various small tasks about the room, the only sound being the soft padding of her unshod feet, and the continued deep growling chant of the old magician. For some ten minutes or so this scene held us silent. Then the old Negro ceased, waved his arms with slow power, when the woman lay down again and became once more rigid. We could detect no sign or sound of breathing in all these minutes. The cloth was restored and the Negro motioned to us to go. We needed no second bidding. I was glad to get outside into the fresh sunlit air. I could not believe what I had seen – definitely enough, an American zombie, a white woman in that occult state, here in Lennox Avenue, Harlem, New York City!

'There!' finished Champley, somewhat nervously, I thought, at the memory of that uncanny episode. 'That is all I can say about this American zombie!'

'There are many tales of the Black Mass in Paris,' I admitted, and mostly it is legend, or something merely theatrical, and with no reality. But what you saw, it seems, had the reality without the ceremony!'

'Since then,' continued the newspaperman, 'I have thought there are perhaps other kinds of zombies. More modern kinds of magic, more modern sorts of delusion? But I must not mingle this occultism with our politics!'

Seeing his Gallic wit reasserting itself, I laughed. I knew that modern Paris held many mysteries, many attractions for princes or paupers, some of them of an occult nature; and some more warmly human in their immediacy of appeal for the ordinary man.

'One thing more,' he reminded himself, 'I never found where this name zombie comes from. They called the woman a *guédé.*'

'Seabrook gives us the name zombie as a Voodoo term, from Haiti,' I ventured. I had heard different names for the same creature in India and Sumatra. 'The word zombie is perhaps from the old Spanish, possibly a corruption of *es hombre* – a man – and *sombre* – a shadow. The Indian name, *chayya,* also means a shadow-creature; but a ghost is a *bhuth*: the double is the *s'arira.*'

These terms do not appear in the standard dictionaries, English or French; nor can they be found even in the occult encyclopaedias. The French word *guède* means woad; while *guerat* means fallow. Does this term then indicate – perhaps as a long-past term of Parisian argot that somehow has reached Haiti – 'the creature that is fallow, incapable of soul-growth'? The island talk of the West Indies has many dialects combining French and Spanish and Portuguese with the African Negro tongues; and newer names have perhaps been found for the ancient and nigh-forgotten magic of the Dark Continent.

THE DROWNED MAN

by Guy de Maupassant

I

EVERYONE in Fécamp knew the story of old Mother Patin. She had undoubtedly been unhappy with her man, had old Mother Patin; for her man had beaten her during his life-time, as a man threshes wheat in his barns.

He was owner of a fishing-smack, and had married her long ago because she was nice, although she was poor.

Patin, a good seaman, but a brute, frequented old Auban's tavern, where, on ordinary days, he drank four or five brandies, and on days when he had made a good catch, eight or ten, and even more, according how he felt, as he said. ·

The brandy was served to customers by old Auban's daughter, a pleasant-faced, dark-haired girl, who drew custom to the house merely by her good looks, for no one had ever wagged a tongue against her.

When Patin entered the tavern, he was content to look at her and talk civilly to her, quiet, decent conversation. When he had drunk the first brandy, already he found her nicer; at the second, he was winking at her; at the third, he was saying: "Miss Désirée, if you would only . . ." without ever finishing the sentence; at the fourth, he was trying to hold her by her petticoat to embrace her; and when he had reached the tenth, it was old Auban who served him with the rest.

The old wine-seller, who knew every trick of the trade, used to send Désirée round between the tables to liven up the orders for drinks; and Désirée, who was not old Auban's daughter for nothing, paraded her petticoat among the drinkers and bandied jests, with a smile on her lips, and a twinkle in her eye.

By dint of drinking brandies, Patin grew so familiar with Désirée's face that he thought of it even at sea, when he threw his nets into the water, out on the open sea, on windy nights and calm nights, on moonlit nights and black nights. He thought of it as he held the helm in the stern of his boat while his four companions slept with their heads on their arms. He saw her always smiling at him, pouring out the yellow brandy with a lift of her shoulders, then coming towards him, saying :

"There! Is this what you want?"

And by dint of treasuring her so in eye and mind, he reached such a pitch of longing to marry her that, unable to restrain himself longer, he asked her in marriage.

He was rich, owner of his boat, his nets and a house at the foot of the cliff, on the Retenue; while old Auban had nothing. He was, therefore, accepted eagerly, and the wedding took place as quickly as possible, both parties being, for different reasons, anxious to make it an accomplished fact.

But three days after the marriage was over, Patin was no longer able to imagine in the least how he had come to think Désirée different from other women. He must have been a rare fool to hamper himself with a penniless girl who had wheedled him with her cognac, so she had, with the cognac into which she had put some filthy drug for him.

And he went cursing along the shore, breaking his pipe between his teeth, swearing at his tackle; and having cursed heartily, with every term he could think of, everything he knew, he spat out the anger still left in his stomach on the fish and crabs that he drew one by one out of his nets, throwing them into the baskets to an accompaniment of oaths and foul words.

Then, returning to his house, where he had his wife, old Auban's daughter, within reach of his tongue and his hand, he soon began to treat her as the lowest of the low. Then, as she listened resignedly, being used to the paternal violence, he became exasperated by her calm, and one evening he beat her. After this, his home became a place of terror.

For ten years, nothing was talked of on the Retenue but the beatings Patin inflicted on his wife, and his habit of cursing when he spoke to her, whatever the occasion. He cursed, in fact, in a unique way, with a wealth of vocabulary and a forceful vigour of delivery possessed by no other man in Fécamp. As soon as his boat reached the harbour mouth, back from fishing, they waited expectantly for the first broadside he would discharge on the pier, from his deck, the moment he saw the white bonnet of his other half.

Standing in the stern, he tacked, his glance fixed ahead and on the sheets when the sea was running high, and in spite of the close attention required by the narrow, difficult passage, in spite of the great waves running mountain-high in the narrow gully, he endeavoured to pick out – from the midst of the women waiting in the spray of the breakers for the sailors – his woman, old Auban's daughter, the pauper wench.

Then, as soon as he saw her, in spite of the clamour of waves and wind, he poured on her a volley of abuse with such vocal energy that every one laughed at it, although they pitied her deeply. Then, when his boat reached the quay, he had a way of discharging his ballast of civilities, as he said, while he unloaded his fish, which attracted round him all the rascals and idlers of the harbour.

It issued from his mouth, now like cannon-shots, terrible and short, now like thunderclaps that rolled for five minutes, such a tempest of oaths that he seemed to have in his lungs all the storms of the Eternal Father.

Then, when he had left his boat, and met among the curious spectators and fishwives, he fished up again from the bottom of the hold a fresh cargo of insults and hard words, and escorted her in such fashion to their home, she in front, he behind, she weeping, he shouting.

Then, alone with her, doors shut, he beat her on the least pretext. Anything was enough to make him lift his hand, and once he had begun, he never stopped, spitting in her face, all the time, the real causes of his hate. At each blow, at each thump, he yelled : "Oh, you penniless slut, oh, you gutter-snipe, oh, you miserable starveling, I did a fine thing the day I washed my mouth out with the firewater of your scoundrel of a father."

She passed her days now, poor woman, in a state of incessant terror, in a continuous trembling of soul and of body, in stunned expectation of insults and thrashings.

And this lasted for ten years. She was so broken that she turned pale when she talked to anyone, no matter who, and no longer thought of anything but the beatings that threatened her, and she had grown as skinny, yellow and dried up as a smoked fish.

II

ONE night when her man was at sea she was awakened by the noise like the growling of a beast which the wind makes when it gets up, like an unleashed hound. She sat up in bed, uneasy, then, hearing nothing more, lay down again; but almost at once, there was a moaning in the chimney that shook the whole house and ran across the whole sky as if a pack of furious animals had crossed the empty spaces panting and bellowing.

Then she got up and ran to the harbour. Other women were running from all sides with lanterns. Men ran up and every one watched the foam flashing white in the darkness on the crest of the waves out at sea.

The storm lasted fifteen hours. Eleven sailors returned no more, and Patin was among them.

The wreckage of his boat, the *Jeune-Amélie*, was recovered off Dieppe. Near Saint-Valéry, they picked up the bodies of his sailors, but his body was never found. As the hull of the small craft had been cut in two, his wife for a long time expected and dreaded his return; for if there had been a collision, it might have happened that the colliding vessel had taken him on board, and carried him to a distant country.

Then, slowly, she grew used to the thought that she was a widow, even though she trembled every time that a neighbour or a beggar or a tramping pedlar entered her house abruptly.

One afternoon, almost four years after the disappearance of her man, she stopped, on her way along the Rue aux Juifs, before the house of an old captain who had died recently, and whose belongings were being sold.

Just at that moment, they were auctioning a parrot, a green parrot with a blue head, which was regarding the crowd with a discontented and uneasy air.

"Three francs," cried the auctioneer, "a bird that talks like a lawyer, three francs."

A friend of Widow Patin jogged her elbow.

"You ought to buy that, you're rich," she said. "It would be company for you; he is worth more than thirty francs, that bird. You can always sell him again for twenty to twenty-five easy."

"Four francs, ladies, four francs," the man repeated. "He sings vespers and preaches like the priest. He's a phenomenon . . . a miracle!"

Widow Patin raised the bid by fifty centimes, and they handed her the hook-nosed creature in a little cage and she carried him off.

Then she installed him in her house, and as she was opening the iron-wire door to give the creature a drink, she got a bite on the finger that broke the skin and drew blood.

"Oh, the wicked bird," said she.

However, she presented him with hemp-seed and maize, then left him smoothing his feathers while he peered with a malicious air at his new home and his new mistress.

Next morning day was beginning to break, when Widow Patin heard, with great distinctness, a loud, resonant, rolling voice. Patin's voice, shouting : "Get up, slut."

Her terror was such that she hid her head under the bedclothes, for every morning, in the old days, as soon as he had opened his eyes, her dead husband shouted in her ears those three familiar words.

Trembling, huddled into a ball, her back turned to the thrashing that she was momentarily expecting, she murmured, her face hidden in the bed :

"God Almighty, he's here! God Almighty, he's here! He's come back, God Almighty!"

Minutes passed; no other sound broke the silence of her room. Then, shuddering, she lifted her head from the bed, sure that he was there, spying on her, ready to strike.

She saw nothing, nothing but a ray of sun falling across the window-pane, and she thought :

"He's hiding, for sure."

She waited a long time, then, a little reassured, thought :

"I must have been dreaming, seeing he doesn't show himself."

She was shutting her eyes again, a little reassured, when right in her ears the furious voice burst out, the thunderous voice of her drowned man, shouting :

"Damn and blast it, get up, you bitch."

She leaped out of bed, jerked out by her instinctive obedience, the passive obedience of a woman broken in by blows, who still remembers, after four years, and will always remember, and always obey that voice. And she said :

"Here I am, Patin. What do you want?"

But Patin did not answer.

Then, bewildered, she looked round her, and searched everywhere, in the cupboards, in the chimney, under the bed, still finding no one, and at last let herself fall into a chair, distracted with misery, convinced that the spirit of Patin itself was there, near her, come back to torture her.

Suddenly, she remembered the loft, which could be reached from outside by a ladder. He had certainly hidden himself there to take her by surprise. He must have been kept by savages on some shore, unable to escape sooner, and he had come back, more wicked than ever. She could not doubt it; the mere tone of his voice convinced her.

She asked, her head turned towards the ceiling :

"Are you up there, Patin?"

Patin did not answer.

Then she went out, and in an utterable terror that set her heart beating madly, she climbed the ladder, opened the garret window, looked in, saw nothing, entered, searched, and found nothing.

Seated on a truss of hay, she began to cry; but while she was sobbing, shaken by an acute and supernatural terror, she heard, in the room below her, Patin telling his story. He seemed less angry, calmer, and he was saying :

"Filthy weather . . . high wind . . . filthy weather. I've had no breakfast, damn it."

She called through the ceiling :

"I'm here, Patin; I'll make you some soup. Don't be angry. I'm coming."

She climbed down at a run.

There was no one in her house.

She felt her body giving way as if Death had his hand on her, and she was going to run out to ask help from the neighbours, when just in her ear the voice cried :

"I've had no breakfast, damn it."

The parrot, in his cage, was watching her with his round, malicious, wicked eye.

She stared back at him in amazement, murmuring :

"Oh, it's you."

He answered, shaking his head :

"Wait, wait, wait, I'll teach you to idle."

What were her thoughts? She felt, she realized that this was none other than the dead man, who had returned and hidden himself in the feathers of this creature, to begin tormenting her again, that he was going to swear, as of old, all day, and find fault with her, and shout insults to attract their neighbours' attention and make them laugh. Then she flung herself across the room, opened the cage, seized the bird, who defended himself and tore her skin with his beak and his claws. But she held him with all her might, in both hands, and throwing herself on the ground, rolled on top of him with mad frenzy, crushed him, made of him a mere rag of flesh, a little, soft, green thing that no longer moved or spoke, and hung limp. Then, wrapping him in a dish-cloth as a shroud, she went out, in her shift, bare-footed, crossed the quay, against which the sea was breaking in small waves, and shaking the cloth, let fall this small, green thing that looked like a handful of grass. Then she returned, threw herself on her knees before the empty cage, and utterly overcome by what she had done, she asked pardon of the good God, sobbing, as if she had just committed a horrible crime.

NIGHT

A NIGHTMARE

By Guy De Maupassant

I love night passionately. I love it as one loves one's country or one's mistress. I love it with all my senses, with my eyes which see it, with my sense of smell which inhales it, with my ears which listen to its silence, with my whole body which is caressed by its shadows. The larks sing in the sunlight, in the blue heavens, in the warm air, in the light air of clear mornings. The owl flies at night, a sombre patch passing through black space, and, rejoicing in the black immensity that intoxicates him, he utters a vibrant and sinister cry.

In the daytime I am tired and bored. The day is brutal and noisy. I rarely get up, I dress myself languidly, and I go out regretfully. Every movement, every gesture, every word, every thought, tires me as though I were raising a crushing load.

But when the sun goes down a confused joy invades my whole being. I awaken and become animated. As the shadows lengthen I feel quite different, younger, stronger, more lively, happier. I watch the great soft shadows falling from the sky and growing deeper. They envelop the city like an impenetrable and impalpable wave; they hide, efface, and destroy colours and forms; they embrace houses, people, and buildings in their imperceptible grasp. Then I would like to cry out with joy like the screech-owls, to run upon the roofs like the cats, and an impetuous, invincible desire to love burns in my veins. I go, I walk, sometimes in the darkened outskirts of Paris, sometimes in the neighbouring woods, where I hear my sisters, the beasts, and my brothers, the poachers, prowling.

One is killed at last by what one loves violently. But how shall I explain what happens to me? How can I ever make people understand that I am able to tell it? I do not know, I cannot tell. I only know that this is—that is all.

Well, yesterday—was it yesterday?—Yes, no doubt, unless it was earlier, a day, a month, a year earlier ... I do not know, but it must have been yesterday, because since then no day has risen, no sun has dawned. But how long has it been night? How long? Who can tell? Who will ever know?

Yesterday, then, I went out after dinner, as I do every evening. It was very fine, very mild, very warm. As I went down towards the boulevards I looked above my head at the black streams full of stars, outlined in the sky between the roofs of the houses, which were turning round and causing this rolling stream of stars to undulate like a real river.

Everything was distinct in the clear air, from the planets to the gas-light. So many lights were burning above, in the city, that the shadows seemed luminous. Bright nights are more joyful than days of bright sunshine. The cafés on the boulevard were flaring; people were laughing, passing up and down, drinking. I went into a theatre for a few moments. Into what theatre, I cannot tell. There was so much light in there that I was depressed, and I came out again with my heart saddened by the clash of brutal light on the gold of the balcony, by the factitious glitter of the great crystal chandelier, by the glaring footlights, by the melancholy of this artificial and crude light. I arrived at the Champs-Elysées, where the open-air concerts look like conflagrations in the branches. The chestnut trees, touched with yellow light, look as if they were painted, like phosphorescent trees. The electric bulbs, like pale dazzling moons, like eggs from the moon, fallen from heaven, like monstrous, living pearls, caused the streaks of gas-light, filthy, ugly gas-light and the garland of coloured, lighted glasses to grow pale beneath their pearly, mysterious, and regal light.

I stopped beneath the Arc de Triomphe to look at the Avenue, the long and wonderful, starry Avenue, leading to Paris between two rows of fire and the stars! The stars above, the unknown stars, thrown haphazard through infinity, where they form those strange shapes which make us dream and think so much.

I entered the Bois de Boulogne, where I remained for a long, long time. I was seized by a strange thrill, a powerful and unforeseen emotion, an exaltation of mind which bordered on frenzy. I walked on and on, and then I returned. What time was it when I passed again beneath the Arc de Triomphe? I do not know. The city was sleeping, and clouds, great black clouds, were slowly spreading over the sky.

For the first time I felt that something strange was going to happen, something new.

It seemed to be getting cold, that the air was becoming thicker, that night, my beloved night, was weighing heavily upon my heart. The Avenue was deserted now. Two solitary policemen were walking near the cab-stand, and a string of vegetable carts was going to the Halles along the roadway, scarcely lit by the gas-jets, which seemed to be dying out. They moved along slowly, laden with carrots, turnips and cabbages. The invisible drivers were asleep, the horses were walking with an even step, following the carts in front of them, and making no noise on the wooden pavement. As they passed each lamp on the footpath, the carrots showed up red in the light, the turnips white, the cabbages green, and they passed one after another, these carts which were as red as fire, as white as silver, and as green as emeralds. I followed them, then I turned into the Rue Royale and returned to the boulevards. There was nobody to be seen, none of the cafés was open; only a few belated pedestrians hurried by. I had never seen Paris so dead and so deserted. I looked at my watch. It was two o'clock.

Some force was driving me, the desire to walk. So I went as far as the Bastille. There I became aware that I had never seen so dark a night, for I could not even see the Colonne de Juillet, whose Genius in gold was lost in the impenetrable obscurity. A curtain of clouds as dense as the ether had buried the stars and seemed to be descending upon the world to blot it out.

I retraced my steps. There was nobody about me. However, at the Place du Château d'Eau, a drunken man almost bumped into me, then disappeared. For some time I could hear his sonorous and uneven steps. I went on. At the top of the Faubourg Montmartre a cab passed, going in the direction of the Seine. I hailed it but the driver did not reply. Near the Rue Drouot a woman was loitering: 'Listen, dearie'—I hastened my steps to avoid her outstretched hand. Then there was nothing more. In front of the Vaudeville Theatre a rag-picker was searching in the gutter. His little lantern was moving just above the ground. I said to him: 'What time is it, my good man?'

'How do I know?' he grumbled. 'I have no watch.'

Then I suddenly perceived that the lamps had all been extinguished. I know that at this time of year they are put out early, before dawn, for the sake of economy. But daylight was still far off, very far off indeed!

'Let us go to the Halles,' I said to myself; 'there at least I shall find life.'

I set off, but it was too dark even to see the way. I advanced slowly, as one does in a forest, recognising the streets by counting them. In front of the Crédit Lyonnais a dog growled. I turned up the Rue de Grammont and lost my way. I wandered about, and then I recognised the Bourse by the iron railings around it. The whole of Paris was sleeping, a deep, terrifying sleep. In the distance a cab rumbled, one solitary cab, perhaps it was the one which had passed me a while back. I tried to reach it, going in the direction of the noise, through streets that were lonely and dark, dark and sombre as death. Again I lost my way. Where was I? What nonsense to put out the lights so soon! Not one person passing by. Not one late reveller, not one thief, not even the mewing of an amorous cat? Nothing.

Where on earth were the police? I said to myself: 'I will shout and they will come.' I shouted. There was no answer. I called more loudly. My voice vanished without an echo, weak, muffled, stifled by the night, the impenetrable night. I yelled: 'Help! Help! Help!' My desperate cry remained unanswered.

What time was it? I pulled out my watch, but I had no matches. I listened to the gentle tick-tick of the little mechanism with a strange and unfamiliar pleasure. It seemed to be a living thing. I felt less lonely. What a mystery. I resumed my walk like a blind man, feeling my way along the wall with my stick, and every moment I raised my eyes to the heavens, hoping that day would dawn at last. But the sky was dark, all dark, more profoundly dark than the city.

What could the time be? It seemed to me I had been walking an infinite length of time, for my legs were giving way beneath me, my breast was heaving, and I was suffering horribly from hunger. I decided to ring at the first street door. I pulled the copper bell and it rang sonorously through the house. It sounded strangely, as if that vibrating noise were alone in the house. I waited. There was no answer. The door did not open. I rang again. I waited again—nothing! I got frightened! I ran to the next house, and, twenty times in succession, I rang the bells in the dark corridors where the concierge was supposed to sleep, but he did not awake. I went on farther, pulling the bells and the knockers with all my strength, kicking and knocking with my hand and stick on the doors, which remained obstinately closed.

Suddenly I perceived that I had reached the Halles. The market was deserted, not a sound, not a movement, not a cart, not a man, not a bundle of flowers or vegetables—it was empty, motionless, abandoned, dead. I was seized with a horrible terror. What was happening? Oh, my God, what was happening?

I set off again. But the time? The time? Who would tell me the time? Not a clock struck in the churches or the public buildings. I thought: 'I will open the glass of my watch and feel the hands with my fingers.' I pulled out my watch.... It was not going.... It had stopped. Nothing more, nothing more, not a ripple in the city, not a light, not the slightest suspicion of a sound in the air. Nothing! Nothing more! not even the distant rumbling of a cab! Nothing more. I had reached the quays, and a cold chill rose from the river. Was the Seine still flowing? I wanted to know, I found the steps and went down. I could not hear the current rushing under the bridge.... A few more steps.... Then sand.... Mud ... then water. I dipped my hand into it. It was flowing ... flowing ... cold ... cold ... cold ... almost frozen ... almost dried up ... almost dead.

I fully realised that I should never have the strength to come up, and that I was going to die there ... in my turn, of hunger, fatigue, and cold.

The Bureau d'Echange de Maux
Lord Dunsany

I often think of the Bureau d'Echange de Maux and the won-
drously evil old man that sat therein. It stood in a little street
that there is in Paris, its doorway made of three brown beams of
wood, the top one overlapping the others like the Greek letter
pai, all the rest painted green, a house far lower and narrower
than its neighbours and infinitely stranger, a thing to take one's
fancy. And over the doorway on the old brown beam in faded
yellow letters this legend ran, 'Bureau Universel d'Echange de
Maux'.

I entered at once and accosted the listless man that lolled on
a stool by his counter. I demanded the wherefore of his wonderful house, what evil wares he exchanged, with many other
things that I wished to know, for curiosity led me: and indeed
had it not I had gone at once from the shop, for there was so
evil a look in that fattened man, in the hang of his fallen cheeks
and his sinful eye, that you would have said he had had dealings
with Hell and won the advantage by sheer wickedness.

Such a man was mine host, but above all the evil of him lay
in his eyes, which lay so still, so apathetic, that you would have
sworn that he was drugged or dead; like lizards motionless on a
wall they lay, then suddenly they darted, and all his cunning
flamed up and revealed itself in what one moment before
seemed no more than a sleepy and ordinary wicked old man.
And this was the object and trade of that peculiar shop, the
Bureau Universel d'Echange de Maux: you paid twenty francs,
which the old man proceeded to take from me, for admission to
the bureau, and then had the right to exchange any evil or
misfortune with anyone on the premises for some evil or misfortune that he 'could afford', as the old man put it.

There were four or five men in the dingy ends of that

74

low-ceilinged room who gesticulated and muttered softly in twos as men who make a bargain, and now and then more came in, and the eyes of the flabby owner of the house leaped up at them as they entered, seemed to know their errands at once and each one's peculiar need, and fell back again into somnolence, receiving his twenty francs in an almost lifeless hand and biting the coin as though in pure absence of mind.

'Some of my clients,' he told me. So amazing to me was the trade of this extraordinary shop that I engaged the old man in conversation, repulsive though he was, and from his garrulity I gathered these facts. He spoke in perfect English though his utterance was somewhat thick and heavy, no language seemed to come amiss to him. He had been in business a great many years, how many he would not say, and was far older than he looked. All kinds of people did business in his shop. What they exchanged with each other he did not care, except that it had to be evils; he was not empowered to carry on any other kind of business.

There was no evil, he told me, that was not negotiable there; no evil the old man knew had ever been taken away in despair from his shop. A man might have to wait and come back again next day and next day and the day after, paying twenty francs each time, but the old man had the addresses of his clients and shrewdly knew their needs, and soon the right two met and eagerly changed their commodities. 'Commodities' was the old man's terrible word, said with a gruesome smack of his heavy lips, for he took a pride in his business and evils to him were goods.

I learned from him in ten minutes very much of human nature, more than I had ever learned from any other man; I learned from him that a man's own evil is to him the worst thing that there is or could be, and that an evil so unbalances all men's minds that they always seek for extremes in that small grim shop. A woman that had no children had exchanged with an impoverished half-maddened creature with twelve. On one occasion a man had exchanged wisdom for folly.

'Why on earth did he do that?' I said.

'None of my business,' the old man answered in his heavy indolent way. He merely took his twenty francs from each and ratified the agreement in the little room at the back opening out of the shop where his clients do business. Apparently the man that had parted with wisdom had left the shop upon the tips of his toes with a happy though foolish expression all over his face, but the other went thoughtfully away wearing a troubled and very puzzled look. Almost always it seemed they did business in opposite evils.

But the thing that puzzled me most in all my talks with that unwieldy man, the thing that puzzles me still, is that none that had once done business in that shop ever returned again; a man might come day after day for many weeks, but once do business and he never returned; so much the old man told me, but, when I asked him why, he only muttered that he did not know.

It was to discover the wherefore of this strange thing, and for no other reason at all, that I determined myself to do business sooner or later in the little room at the back of that mysterious shop. I determined to exchange some very trivial evil for some evil equally slight, to seek for myself an advantage so very small as scarcely to give Fate as it were a grip; for I deeply distrusted these bargains, knowing well that man has never yet benefited by the marvellous and that the more miraculous his advantage appears to be the more securely and tightly do the gods or the witches catch him. In a few days more I was going back to England and I was beginning to fear that I should be sea-sick: this fear of sea-sickness, not the actual malady but only the mere fear of it, I decided to exchange for a suitably little evil. I did not know with whom I should be dealing, who in reality was the head of the firm (one never does when shopping), but I decided that neither Jew nor Devil could make very much on so small a bargain as that.

I told the old man my project, and he scoffed at the smallness of my commodity, trying to urge me on to some darker bargain, but could not move me from my purpose. And then he told me tales with a somewhat boastful air of the big business, the great bargains, that had passed through his hands. A man had once run in there to try and exchange death; he had swallowed poison by accident and had only twelve hours to live. That sinister old man had been able to oblige him. A client was willing to exchange the commodity.

'But what did he give in exchange for death?' I said.

'Life,' said that grim old man with a furtive chuckle.

'It must have been a horrible life,' I said.

'That was not my affair,' the proprietor said, lazily rattling together as he spoke a little pocketful of twenty-franc pieces.

Strange business I watched in that shop for the next few days, the exchange of odd commodities, and heard strange mutterings in corners amongst couples who presently rose and went to the back room, the old man following to ratify.

Twice a day for a week I paid my twenty francs, watching life with its great needs and its little needs morning and afternoon spread out before me in all its wonderful variety.

And one day I met a comfortable man with only a little need, he seemed to have the very evil I wanted. He always feared the lift was going to break. I knew too much of hydraulics to fear things as silly as that, but it was not my business to cure his ridiculous fear. Very few words were needed to convince him that mine was the evil for him, he never crossed the sea, and I, on the other hand, could always walk upstairs, and I also felt at the time, as many must feel in that shop, that so absurd a fear could never trouble me. And yet at times it is almost the curse of my life. When we both had signed the parchment in the spidery back room and the old man had signed and ratified (for which we had to pay him fifty francs each) I went back to my hotel, and there I saw the deadly thing in the basement. They asked me if I would go upstairs in the lift; from force of habit I risked it, and I held my breath all the way up and clenched my hands. Nothing will induce me to try such a journey again. I would sooner go up to my room in a balloon. And why? Because if a balloon goes wrong you have a chance, it may spread out into a parachute after it has burst, it may catch in a tree, a hundred and one things may happen, but if the lift falls down its shaft you are done. As for sea-sickness I shall never be sick again, I cannot tell you why except that I know that it is so.

And the shop in which I made this remarkable bargain, the shop to which none return when their business is done: I set out for it next day. Blindfold I could have found my way to the unfashionable quarter out of which a mean street runs, where you take the alley at the end, whence runs the cul-de-sac where the queer shop stood. A shop with pillars, fluted and painted red, stands on its near side, its other neighbour is a low-class jeweller's with little silver brooches in the window. In such incongruous company stood the shop with beams, with its walls painted green.

In half an hour I stood in the cul-de-sac to which I had gone twice a day for the last week. I found the shop with the ugly painted pillars and the jeweller that sold brooches, but the green house with the three beams was gone.

Pulled down, you will say, although in a single night. That can never be the answer to the mystery, for the house of the fluted pillars painted on plaster, and the low-class jeweller's shop with its silver brooches (all of which I could identify one by one) were standing side by side.

THE MUMMY'S FOOT

by *Théophile Gautier*

I had entered, in an idle mood, the shop of one of those curiosity vendors who are called *marchands de bric-à-brac* in that Parisian argot which is so perfectly unintelligible elsewhere in France.

The warehouse of my *bric-à-brac* dealer was a veritable Capharnaum; all ages and all nations seemed to have made their rendezvous there; an Etruscan lamp of red clay stood upon a Boule cabinet, with ebony panels, brightly striped by lines of inlaid brass; a duchess of the court of Louis XV nonchalantly extended her fawn-like feet under a massive table of the time of Louis XIII with heavy spiral supports of oak, and carven designs of chimeras and foliage intermingled.

From disembowelled cabinets escaped cascades of silver-lustrous Chinese silks and waves of tinsel, which an oblique sunbean shot through with luminous beads; while portraits of every era, in frames more or less tarnished, smiled through their yellow varnish.

The dealer followed me closely through the tortuous way contrived between the piles of furniture.

It was a singular face, that of the merchant. An immense skull, polished like a knee, and surrounded by a thin aureole of white hair, which brought out the clear salmon tint of his complexion all the more strikingly, lent him a false aspect of patriarchal *bonhomie*, counteracted, however, by the scintillation of two little yellow eyes which trembled in their orbits like two louis d'or upon quicksilver.

The curve of his nose presented an aquiline silhouette

which suggested the Oriental or Jewish type. His hands – thin, slender, full of nerves which projected like strings upon the finger-board of a violin, and armed with claws like those on the terminations of bats' wings – shook with senile trembling; but those convulsively agitated hands became firmer than steel pincers or lobsters' claws when they lifted any precious article – an onyx cup, a Venetian glass, or a dish of Bohemian crystal. This strange old man had an aspect so thoroughly rabbinical and cabalistic that he would have been burnt on the mere testimony of his face three centuries ago.

'Will you not buy something from me to-day, sir? Here is a Malay kreese with blade undulating like flame; look at those grooves contrived for the blood to run along – it is a fine character of ferocious arm, and will look well in your collection: this two-handed sword is very beautiful – it is the work of Josepe de la Hera; and this *colichemarde*, with its fenestrated guard – what a superb specimen of handicraft!'

'No; I have quite enough weapons and instruments of carnage – I want a small figure, something which will suit me as a paper-weight; for I cannot endure those trumpery bronzes which the stationers sell, and which may be found on everybody's desk.'

The old gnome foraged among his ancient wares, and finally arranged before me some antique bronzes – so-called, at least; fragments of malachite; little Hindoo or Chinese idols – a kind of poussah toys in jade-stone, representing the incarnations of Brahma or Vishnoo, and wonderfully appropriate to the very undivine office of holding papers and letters in place.

I was hesitating between a porcelain dragon, all constellated with warts – its mouth formidable with bristling tusks and ranges of teeth – and an abominable little Mexican fetish, representing the god Zitziliputzi *au naturel*, when I caught sight of a charming foot, which I at first took for a fragment of some antique Venus.

It had those beautiful ruddy and tawny tints that lend to Florentine bronze that warm living look so much preferable to the grey-green aspect of common bronzes, which might easily be mistaken for statues in a state of putrefaction:

satiny gleams played over its rounded forms, doubtless polished by the amorous kisses of twenty centuries.

'That foot will be my choice,' I said to the merchant, who regarded me with an ironical and saturnine air, and held out the object desired that I might examine it more fully.

I was surprised at its lightness; it was not a foot of metal, but in sooth a foot of flesh – an embalmed foot – a mummy's foot: on examining it still more closely the very grain of the skin, and the almost imperceptible lines impressed upon it by the texture of the bandages, became perceptible.

The toes were slender and delicate, and terminated by perfectly formed nails, pure and transparent as agates; the great toe, slightly separated from the rest, afforded a happy contrast, in the antique style to the position of the other toes, and lent it an aerial lightness – the grace of a bird's foot – the sole, scarcely streaked by a few almost imperceptible cross lines, afforded evidence that it had never touched the bare ground, and had only come in contact with the finest matting of Nile rushes, and the softest carpets of panther skin.

'Ha, ha! – You want the foot of the Princess Hermonthis,' exclaimed the merchant, with a strange giggle, fixing his owlish eyes upon me. 'Ha, ha, ha! For a paper-weight! An original idea! Artistic idea! Old Pharaoh would certainly have been surprised had someone told him that the foot of his adored daughter would be used for a paper-weight after he had had a mountain of granite hollowed out as a receptacle for the triple coffin, painted and gilded – covered with hieroglyphics and beautiful paintings of the Judgment of Souls,' continued the queer little merchant, half audibly, as though talking to himself.

'How much will you charge me for this mummy fragment?'

'Ah, the highest price I can get; for it is a superb piece.'

'Assuredly that is not a common article; but, still, how much do you want? In the first place let me warn you that all my wealth consists of just five louis: I can buy anything that costs five louis, but nothing dearer.'

'Five louis for the foot of the Princess Hermonthis! That is very little, very little indeed; 'tis an authentic foot,' muttered the merchant, shaking his head, and imparting a peculiar rotary motion in his eyes. 'Well, take it, and I will give you the bandages into the bargain,' he added, wrapping the foot in an ancient damask rag.

He poured the gold coins into a sort of mediæval alms-purse hanging at his belt, repeating: 'The foot of the Princess Hermonthis, to be used for a paper-weight!'

Then, turning his phosphorescent eyes upon me, he exclaimed in a voice strident as the crying of a cat which has swallowed a fishbone: 'Old Pharaoh will not be well pleased; he loved his daughter – the dear man!'

'You speak as if you were a contemporary of his: you are old enough, goodness knows! but you do not date back to the Pyramids of Egypt,' I answered, laughingly, from the threshold.

I went home, delighted with my acquisition.

With the idea of putting it to profitable use as soon as possible, I placed the foot of the divine Princess Hermonthis upon a heap of papers scribbled over with verses, in themselves an undecipherable mosaic work of erasures; articles freshly begun; letters forgotten. The effect was charming, bizarre, and romantic.

Well satisfied with this embellishment, I went out with the gravity and pride becoming one who feels that he has the ineffable advantage over all the passers-by whom he elbows, of possessing a piece of the Princess Hermonthis, daughter of Pharaoh.

I looked upon all who did not possess, like myself, a paper-weight so authentically Egyptian, as very ridiculous people; and it seemed to me that the proper occupation of every sensible man should consist in the mere fact of having a mummy's foot upon his desk.

Happily I met some friends whose presence distracted me in my infatuation with this new acquisition: I went to dinner with them.

When I came back that evening, with my brain slightly confused by a few glasses of wine, a vague whiff of Oriental perfume delicately titillated my olfactory nerves; the heat of the room had warmed the natron, bitumen, and myrrh in which the *paraschistes*, who cut open the bodies of the dead, had bathed the corpse of the princess; it was a perfume at once sweet and penetrating – a perfume that four thousand years had not been able to dissipate.

I soon drank deeply from the black cup of sleep: for a few hours all remained opaque to me.

Yet light gradually dawned upon the darkness of my mind; dreams commenced to touch me softly in their silent flight.

The eyes of my soul were opened; and I beheld my chamber as it actually was; I might have believed myself awake but for a vague consciousness which assured me that I slept and that something fantastic was about to take place.

The odour of the myrrh had augmented in intensity: and I felt a slight headache, which I very naturally attributed to several glasses of champagne that we had drunk to the unknown gods and our future fortunes.

I peered through my room with a feeling of expectation which I saw nothing to justify: every article of furniture was in its proper place.

After a few moments, however, all this calm interior appeared to become disturbed; the woodwork cracked stealthily; the ash-covered log suddenly emitted a jet of blue flame.

My eyes accidentally fell upon the desk where I had placed the foot of the Princess Hermonthis.

Instead of remaining quiet – as behoved a foot which had been embalmed for four thousand years – it commenced to act in a nervous manner; contracted itself, and leaped over the papers like a startled frog. One would have imagined that it had suddenly been brought into contact with a galvanic battery: I could distinctly hear the dry sound made by its little heel, hard as the hoof of a gazelle.

Suddenly I saw the folds of my bed-curtain stir, and heard a bumping sound, like that caused by some person hopping on one foot across the floor. I must confess I became alternately hot and cold; that I felt a strange wind chill my back.

The bed-curtains opened and I beheld the strangest figure imaginable before me.

It was a young girl of a very deep coffee-brown complexion, like the bayadere Amani, and possessing the purest Egyptian type of perfect beauty: her eyes were almond shaped and oblique, with eyebrows so black that they seemed blue; her nose was exquisitely chiselled, almost Greek in its delicacy of outline; and she might indeed have been taken for a

Corinthian statue of bronze but for the prominence of her cheekbones and the slightly African fullness of her lips.

Her arms, slender and spindle-shaped, like those of very young girls, were encircled by a peculiar kind of metal bands and bracelets of glass beads; her hair was all twisted into little cords, and she wore upon her bosom a little idol-figure of green paste, bearing a whip with seven lashes, which proved it to be an image of Isis. Her brow was adorned with a shining plate of gold, and a few traces of paint relieved the coppery tint of her cheeks.

As for her costume, it was very odd indeed.

Fancy a *pagne* or skirt all formed of little strips of material bedizened with red and black hieroglyphics, stiffened with bitumen, and apparently belonging to a freshly unbandaged mummy.

In one of those sudden flights of thought so common in dreams I heard the hoarse falsetto of the *bric-à-brac* dealer repeating like a monotonous refrain the phrase he had uttered in his shop with so enigmatical an intonation:

'Old Pharaoh will not be well pleased: he loved his daughter, the dear man!'

One strange circumstance, which was not at all calculated to restore my equanimity, was that the apparition had but one foot; the other was broken off at the ankle!

She approached the table where the foot was starting and fidgeting about more than ever, and there supported herself upon the edge of the desk. I saw her eyes fill with pearly-gleaming tears.

Although she had not as yet spoken, I fully comprehended the thoughts which agitated her: she looked at her foot – for it was indeed her own – with an exquisitely graceful expression of coquettish sadness; but the foot leaped and ran hither and thither, as though impelled on steel springs.

Then commenced between the Princess Hermonthis and her foot – which appeared to be endowed with a special life of its own – a very fantastic dialogue in a most ancient Coptic tongue, such as might have been spoken thirty centuries ago in the syrinxes of the land of Ser: luckily, I understood Coptic perfectly well that night.

The Princess Hermonthis cried, in a voice sweet and vibrant as the tones of a crystal bell:

'Well, my dear little foot, you always flee from me; yet I always took good care of you, I bathed you with perfumed water in a bowl of alabaster; I smoothed your heel with pumice-stone mixed with palm oil; your nails were cut with golden scissors and polished with a hippopotamus tooth; I was careful to select *tatbebs* for you, painted and embroidered and turned up at the toes, which were the envy of all the young girls in Egypt: you wore on your toe rings bearing the device of the sacred scarabæus; and you supported one of the lightest bodies that a lazy foot could sustain.'

The foot replied, in a pouting and chagrined tone:

'You know well that I do not belong to myself any longer – I have been bought and paid for; the old merchant knew what he was about; he bore you a grudge for having refused to espouse him; – this is an ill turn which he has done you. The Arab who violated your royal coffin in the subterranean pits of the necropolis of Thebes was sent thither by him: he desired to prevent you from being present at the reunion of the shadowy nations in the cities below. Have you five pieces of gold for my ransom?'

'Alas, no! – my jewels, my rings, my purses of gold and silver, they were all stolen from me,' answered the Princess Hermonthis, with a sob.

'Princess,' I then exclaimed, 'I never retained anybody's foot unjustly; even though you have not got the five louis which it cost me, I present it to you gladly: I should feel unutterably wretched to think that I were the cause of so amiable a person as the Princess Hermonthis being lame.'

She turned a look of deepest gratitude upon me; and her eyes shone with bluish gleams of light.

She took her foot – which surrendered itself willingly this time – like a woman about to put on her little shoe, and adjusted it to her leg with much skill.

This operation over, she took a few steps about the room, as though to assure herself that she was really no longer lame.

'Ah, how pleased my father will be! – he who was so unhappy because of my mutilation, and who from the moment of my birth set a whole nation at work to hollow me out a tomb so deep that he might preserve me intact until that last day when souls must be weighed in the balance of Amenthi! Come with me to my father; he will receive you kindly, for you have given me back my foot.'

I thought this proposition natural enough. I arrayed myself in a dressing-gown of large-flowered pattern, which lent me a very Pharanoic aspect; hurriedly put on a pair of Turkish slippers, and informed the Princess Hermonthis that I was ready to follow her.

Before starting, Hermonthis took from her neck the little idol of green paste, and laid it on the scattered sheets of paper which covered the table.

'It is only fair,' she observed smilingly, 'that I should re-place your paper-weight.'

She gave me her hand, which felt soft and cold, like the skin of a serpent; and we departed.

We passed for some time with the velocity of an arrow through a fluid and greyish expanse, in which half-formed silhouettes flitted swiftly by us, to right and left.

For an instant we saw only sky and sea.

A few moments later obelisks commenced to tower in the distance: pylons and vast flights of steps guarded by sphinxes became clearly outlined against the horizon.

We had reached our destination.

The princess conducted me to the mountain of rose-coloured granite, in the face of which appeared an opening so narrow and low that it would have been difficult to distinguish it from the fissures in the rock had not its location been marked by two stelæ wrought with sculptures.

Hermonthis kindled a torch, and led the way before me.

We traversed corridors hewn through the living rock: their walls, covered with hieroglyphics and paintings of allegorical processions, might well have occupied thousands of arms for thousands of years in their formation; these corridors, of interminable length, opened into square chambers, in the midst of which pits had been contrived, through which we descended by cramp-irons or spiral stair-ways; these pits again conducted us into other chambers, opening into other corridors, likewise decorated with painted sparrow-hawks, serpents coiled in circles.

At last we found ourselves in a hall so vast, so enormous, so immeasurable, that the eye could not reach its limits; files of monstrous columns stretched far out of sight on every side, between which winked livid stars of yellowish flame.

The Princess Hermonthis still held my hand, and graciously saluted the mummies of her acquaintance.

My eyes became accustomed to the dim twilight, and objects became discernible.

I beheld the kings of the subterranean races seated upon thrones – grand old men, though dry, withered, wrinkled like parchment, and blackened with naphtha and bitumen – all wearing *pshents* of gold, and breastplates and gorgets glittering with precious stones; their eyes immovably fixed like the eyes of sphinxes, and their long beards whitened by the snow of centuries. Behind them stood their peoples, in the stiff and constrained posture enjoined by Egyptian art, all eternally preserving the attitude prescribed by the hieratic code. Behind these nations, the cats, ibises, and crocodiles contemporary with them – rendered monstrous of aspect by their swathing bands – mewed, flapped their wings, or extended their jaws in a saurian giggle.

All the Pharaohs were there – Cheops, Chephrenes, Psammetichus, Sesostris, Amenotaph – all the dark rulers of the pyramids and syrinxes; on yet higher thrones sat Chronos and Xixouthros – who was contemporary with the deluge; and Tubal Cain, who reigned before it.

The beard of King Xixouthros had grown seven times around the granite table upon which he leaned, lost in deep reverie – and buried in dreams.

Further back, through a dusty cloud, I beheld dimly the seventy-two pre-Adamite Kings, with their seventy-two peoples – forever passed away.

After permitting me to gaze upon this bewildering spectacle a few moments, the Princess Hermonthis presented me to her father Pharaoh, who favoured me with a most gracious nod.

'I have found my foot again! I have found my foot!' cried the Princess, clapping her little hands together with every sign of frantic joy. 'It was this gentleman who restored it to me.'

The races of Kemi, the races of Nahasi – all the black, bronzed, and copper-coloured nations – repeated in chorus:

'The Princess Hermonthis has found her foot again!'

Even Xixouthros himself was visibly affected.

He raised his heavy eyelids, stroked his moustache with his fingers, and turned upon me a glance weighty with centuries.

'By Oms, the dog of Hell, and Tmei, daughter of the Sun and of Truth, this is a brave and worthy lad!' explained Pharaoh, pointing to me with his sceptre, which was terminated with a lotus-flower.

'What recompense do you desire?'

Filled with that daring inspired by dreams in which nothing seems impossible, I asked him for the hand of the Princess Hermonthis; the hand seemed to me a very proper antithetic recompense for the foot.

Pharaoh opened wide his great eyes of glass in astonishment at my witty request.

'What country do you come from? And what is your age?'

'I am a Frenchman; and I am twenty-seven years old, venerable Pharaoh.'

'Twenty-seven years old! And he wishes to espouse the Princess Hermonthis who is thirty centuries old!' cried out at once all the Thrones and all the Circles of Nations.

Only Hermonthis herself did not seem to think my request unreasonable.

'If you were even only two thousand years old,' replied the ancient King, 'I would willingly give you the Princess; but the disproportion is too great; and, besides, we must give our daughters husbands who will last well; you do not know how to preserve yourself any longer; even those who died only fifteen centuries ago are already no more than a handful of dust; behold, my flesh is solid as basalt; my bones are bars of steel!

'I shall be present on the last day of the world, with the same body and the same features which I had during my lifetime; my daughter Hermonthis will last longer than a statue of bronze.

'Then the last particles of your dust will have been scattered abroad by the winds; and even Isis herself, who was able to find the atoms of Osiris, would scarce be able to recompose your being.

'See how vigorous I yet remain, and how mighty is my

grasp,' he added, shaking my hand in the English fashion with a strength that buried my rings in the flesh of my fingers.

He squeezed me so hard that I awoke, and found my friend Alfred shaking me by the arm to make me get up.

'O you everlasting sleeper! Must I have you carried out into the middle of the street, and fireworks exploded in your ears? It is after noon; don't you recollect your promise to take me with you to see M Aguado's Spanish pictures?'

'God! I forgot all, all about it,' I answered, dressing myself hurriedly; 'we will go there at once; I have the permit lying on my desk.'

I started to find it – but fancy my astonishment when I beheld, instead of the mummy's foot I had purchased the evening before, the little green paste idol left in its place by the Princess Hermonthis!

S IR WILLIAM TEMPLE'S observation is in one respect at least just, for in France the belief in werewolfism has certainly survived, and the tradition descends unbroken from the very dawn of history. Shape-shifting (as has already been remarked) was part and parcel of the wizard lore of the Druids, of whose sacred shrines none was more secret and more evil than the little isle of Sain, off Finistère, near " le Ras de Fontenay ", so infamous for shipwrecks, an eyot dedicated to He'ro Dias, the mistress of witches.   There dwelt nine fearful beldames, ministers of the demon oracle of " Sena ", the Hag ; " Gallizenas uocant," says Pomponius Mela, who attributes to them evil powers of brewing storms and peering into futurity, but above all, " seque in quae uelint animalia uertere," and they ken full subtily to change themselves into the shapes of whatsoever animals they list.[1]

As of old upon Mount Carmel the sorcerer bishops of Baal withstood the prophet Elias, so the devotees of dark heathen rites battled in Britain and in Gaul against the holy evangel, and very many are the existing records of the contests between the Druid colleges or devilish covens and the Saints of God.[2] As may be supposed, the warlock host set in motion the whole thaumaturgy and sleeveless machinery of hell to prevent and eclipse the miracles of the Saints, and of course contended frustrate and in vain.

" This man casteth not out devils but by Beelzebub the prince of the devils," quoth the Pharisees.   " If they have called the goodman of the house Beelzebub, how much more them of his household ? "[3] That charges should be brought against the enemies of the demon was but to be expected.   Thus Saint Ronan was maligned by certain evil men, professing Christians but in their hearts ethnic and profane. This great Saint was a native of Ireland, and a disciple of S. Senan in Scatling Island.   He followed his

THE WEREWOLF

preceptor to Cornwall and thence to Brittany, where settling in the vicinity of Leon, about the year 510 he founded Locronan. He died near Hillian on the Anse d'Iffignac, Domnonia, in 540. At Locronan his Feast is on the Second Sunday in July ; at Tavistock in Devon on 30th August. A Feast of the Translation of his Relics is observed on 5th January.[4] Now the evil and envious eyes of certain unrighteous, amongst whom was a sinful woman named Keban, could not bear but were dazzled by the splendour of the virtues and piety of S. Ronan, wherefore they most wickedly and lyingly made plaint to King Grallon, who then with all his following held high court at Kemper, that S. Ronan was a varlet and a warlock foul, and that, even as the dreaded werewolves of old, by art, magic, and black cantrips not a few, he would often change himself into a brute beast, ay, into a raging wolf, and so guised he was wont to prowl abroad and raven through the countryside. Moreover, in the malice of her heart Keban averred that her child had been devoured by a wolf, the same savage beast who marauded the flocks and herds, and that S. Ronan was this very wolf. The Saint, however, easily cleared himself of the foul charge, and in his charity not only forgave, but (it is said) converted his enemies.

Werewolfism was a very terrible and real thing, a sorcery which, as we have already seen from Gervase of Tilbury, persisted through the centuries. In his *Origines Gauloises*,[6] La Tour-D'Auvergne-Corret, writing of the period following the introduction of Christianity into Gaul, says that from pagan times a certain occultism and witchcrafts were maintained for many generations. Although the Bretons are truly enlightened by the Catholic Faith and very devout, there yet endure in dark corners goetic practices and necromancies. There are, and there have always been, impious men so lost and abandoned that they do not hesitate to make pacts with the prince of evil in order to acquire temporal advantage and supernatural powers. Many of these warlocks, the Bretons relate, either dress themselves at night in wolf-skins, or assume the shape of wolves in order to repair to these assemblies over which Satan (it is averred) presides in person. These masqueradings or shape-shifting of the men-wolves, a craft descending from the

LE MENEU' DE LOUPS
By Maurice Sand (See p. 237)

earliest days of ancient Armonica, may be fitly compared with what history tells us of the Irish lycanthropes as also with the werewolfery recorded by Herodotus, Pliny, and other classical authors.

In 1181, Hugues de Camp-d'Avesnes, Comte de Saint-Pol, attacked and burned to the ground the Abbey of Saint-Riquier, where two of his enemies, the Comte d'Auxi and the Comte de Beaurain-sur-Canche, had taken refuge with their followers. In the pillage and the fire on 28th July nearly three thousand persons perished. Some few, including the Abbot, hardly escaped to Abbeville. Hugues de Saint-Pol, in spite of the Abbot's complaint, continued to ravage Ponthieu, but he reckoned without Louis-le-Gros, who soon let him learn that he intended to take the field and avenge the massacre. In terror Hugues threw himself at the feet of Innocent II, but the Pontiff, aghast at the sacrilege, held out litle hope of pardon, at least the culprit must expect to dree a long a weary weird. The Count, however, founded the Abbey of Cercamp, richly endowing it as a reparation. Nevertheless after his death he was doomed for many centuries to haunt the district he had so cruelly ravaged. He was seen nightly prowling near the Abbey of Saint-Riquier, a horrible phantom, black and loaded with chains, in the form of a wolf, howling most piteously. Sometimes this terrible spectre even invaded the streets of Abbeville, where it was known as *la bête Canteraine*.[7]

The famous lay *Bisclavret*,[8] by that sweet and gracious poetess Marie de France, who dedicated her collected work to our King Henry II, shows that she had very considerable knowledge of the traditional craft of werewolfery, and affords so many interesting details that it must certainly be briefly mentioned here. *Bisclavret* is the Breton term for the Norman *Garulf*, werewolf.

> Bisclavret a nun en Bretan,
> Garulf l'apelent li Norman.
> Jadis le poeit hum oïr
> e sovent suleit avenir,
> hume plusur garulf devindrent
> e es boscages maisun tindrent.
> Garulf, ceo est beste salvage ;
> tant cum il est en cele rage,
> humes devure, grant mal fait,
> es granz forez converse e vait.

Bisclavret tells of a great lord of Brittany, wealthy and much honoured, who dearly loved and was loved by his wife. One thing, however, troubled her. For three days each week he privily leaves his home and never explains these absences. By much cajolery his wife persuades him to confess that during these three days he becomes a werewolf, and roves in the depths of the forest living by violence and blood, " de preie et de ravine." He is stark naked at the time of the metamorphosis. He even confides to her where he closets his clothes, under a stone in an ancient hermitage, but this secret he only tells after much coaxing, since if he cannot recover this same attire upon his return to the spot he will be doomed always to remain a wolf. The lady, filled with fear, dissembles, but soon persuades a certain knight, who has long loved her, to search out the clothes and steal them away, so that her lord can never recover human shape. This done, she marries her lover and they enjoy the werewolf's riches and estates. Eventually the plot is discovered, and the Bisclavret is enabled to transform himself into a man, since the apparel has been fortunately preserved.

Passing mention may here perhaps not impertinently be made of the *Roman de Guillaume de Palerme*, which was translated from the French by the command of Sir Humphrey de Bohun about 1350 as *The Romance of William of Palerne*, otherwise known as *William and the Werwolf*.[9] The original tale was in its day immensely popular, although apparently only one MS. has been preserved. Skeat dates the composition as between 1178 and 1200. At the beginning of the sixteenth century the poem was turned into French prose. The story is one of long and complicated incident. Embrons, King of Apulia, and his wife Felice, daughter of the Emperor of Greece, have a fair son named William, who whilst he is at play (at Palermo) is caught by a wolf, with wide, gaping jaws, " un grans leus, goule baee." This animal swims the sea with him to Italy and carries him to a forest near Rome, where it tends and feeds him. This wolf was actually a werewolf, Alphonsus, heir to the crown of Spain, who had been thus ensorcelled by his stepmother Braunde, so that her son Braundinis might succeed.

la nuit le couche joste soi ;
li leus-garous le fil le roi
lacole de ses iiii pies.
si est de lui aprivoisies,
li fix le roi, que tot li plaist
ce que la beste de lui fait.[10]

However, whilst the werewolf is away seeking food, a cowherd finds the child and adopts him. The Emperor of Rome one day whilst hunting meets William, who so pleases him that he appoints the boy as page to his daughter Melior. Presently the young couple are in love, and as the Emperor of Greece sends to ask the hand of Melior for Prince Partendon, his son, they escape, sewn up in the skins of two white bears. Thus disguised they wander in the forest, and are found by the werewolf who succours the truant pair. They reach Benevento, and only elude capture by the werewolf's aid. Next they dress up as a hart and hind, and with the werewolf reach Sicily. Palermo is besieged by the Spaniards, since the King of Spain seeks the hand of Florence (William's sister) for Prince Braundinis and has been refused. At the request of Queen Felice, his mother, William joins battle against the Spaniards, and when she asks what cognizance he will have on his shield, he demands a werewolf shall be painted there :—

" i coueyte nought elles
but that I haue a god schel[d] · of gold graithed clene,
& wel & faire with-inne · a werwolf depeynted,
that be hidous & huge · to haue alle his rightes,
of the couenablest colour · to knowe in the feld ;
other armes al my lif · atteli neuer haue." [11]

Thus armed William performs doughty deeds, takes the King of Spain and his son prisoners, and routs the foe. Wicked Queen Braunde is sent for and forced to dissolve the charm, so Prince Alphonsus recovers his human shape. It appears that the good werewolf stole William to save him from the plots of King Embrons' brother, who coveted the sceptre of Sicily. William marries Melior ; Alphonsus, soon to be King of Spain, weds Florence. A little while, and the Emperor of Rome dying, William is crowned Emperor with great pomp and ceremony.

The narrative is most excellently told, but it will be understood that I have only been able to touch upon a few of the crowding incidents, and many characters and episodes I have necessarily omitted.

In the Middle Ages it was often believed that if any person had been denounced from the altar and remained impenitent, refusing to make restitution and confess, the curse of the werewolf fell upon him. In Normandy any man who was excommunicate became a werewolf for a term of three or seven years. In Basse-Bretagne any person who had not been shriven for ten years nor used holy water could become a werewolf. This belief was still current in the middle of the eighteenth century. In La Vendée the man who was excommunicate became a werewolf for seven years, during which he was obliged to haunt certain ill-omened and accursed spots.[12]

William of Auvergne, Bishop of Paris, who died in 1249, in his *De Universo*,[13] pars. II, iii, cap. 13 : *Qualiter maligni spiritus uexant, et decipiunt homines*, treats of diabolical werewolfism at some length, and tells of a demoniac, possessed by an evil spirit, who drove him out into some secret and privy place, there leaving him as dead. Meanwhile the demon entered into a wolf, or it may be assumed the form of a ravening wolf, and rushed abroad into the village street and lanes, howling fearfully, snapping and rending with his teeth, so that all were horribly afraid and amazed at this monster of hell. The story soon went forth that this man was a werewolf. Moreover, the man himself believed that he was changed into a very wolf, that wolf which filled the whole countryside with panic and alarm. It happened that a holy religious heard the rumour, and presently he came to the village where these things were wrought, and calling together the good folk he told them plainly that this man was not essentially metamorphosed into a wolf, as all believed. By divine inspiration he even led them to the spot where the man lay entranced, as one dead, and showed him thus to the people. The religious then awoke him, and even commanded the wolf to show himself, which the beast did howling. He then exorcized the man and forever freed him from this ensorcellment of Satan.

Wherefore, says the good bishop, we find that in this instance at least the Devil impressed the imaginative faculty of the men with the idea that he was a wolf. Nevertheless, his essential part, his soul, never entered nor could enter into the body of a wolf, although deluded by the demon he steadfastly conceived such to have been the case. In chapter 23 of the same work he discusses the glamour caused by the Devil and magic crafts—*ludificationes daemonum.*

" It is like the sin of witchcraft, to rebel," and it can surprise nobody that throughout the sixteenth century, when all hell stirred to its depth to lash to fury the hoaming sea of infidelity and schisms that surged and roared round the Rock of Peter, there was an almost unprecedented eagre of sorcery and evil. To-day, as of old, in many a European country, rebellion and revolt against God and the ordinances of God are being crutched by Satanism. Four hundred years ago England was ravaged by the dissolution of her religious houses ; France was rent and torn by the horrors of intestine war.

It is during the sixteenth century that in France especially the rank foul weeds of werewolfery flourished exceedingly.

In December, 1521, at Poligny, Pierre Burgot, known as " Gros Pierre ", and Michel Verdun were tried before Maître Jean Boin, O.P., S.T.D., Prior of the Dominican convent at Poligny and Inquisitor General for the diocese of Besançon. Day after day the Court was thronged. Pierre Burgot confessed that nineteen years before, on the day of Poligny Fair, whilst owing to a great storm of thunder and hail he was collecting his flocks, there met him in a lonely place three horsemen clothed in black, riding black steeds. Of these one accosted him asking what ailed him. He replied his flocks were lost and he feared lest they should fall a prey to wild beasts. The man—or rather demon—then said that if he would acknowledge and serve him as his lord and master not one sheep should be missing. He accepted the proposal and agreed to meet him a sennight after to seal the bond. This he did, and kneeling before the demon in homage, vowed to obey him, renouncing God, Our Lady, all the Company of Heaven, his Baptism and Chrism. He swore also never to assist at Holy Mass, nor yet to use Holy Water. He then kissed the demon's left hand, which was black, and cold as the hand of a corpse. The demon promised Pierre money, and bade the shepherd call upon him by the name of Moyset. Howbeit as the years went by he grew weary of his allegiance, to which he was recalled by Michel Verdun of Plane, a village near Poligny, and he attended a sabbat of warlocks in a wood near Château Charlou. Michel bade him strip naked and then anointed him from head to foot with a certain unguent, after which he seemed to himself to be changed into a wolf, his limbs were hairy, his hands and feet the paws of a beast. In running his speed was that of the wind. Michel, who also shifted his shape, accompanied him with surpassing fleetness. The unguent was given to Pierre by Moyset ; and to Michel Verdun by his familiar, Guillemin. After these courses Pierre felt an intense weariness.

In the shape of wolves Pierre and Michel attacked and tore to pieces a boy of seven years old. An outcry was raised and they fled. On another occasion they killed a woman who was gathering peas. They also seized a little girl of four years old and ate the palpitating flesh, all save one arm. Several other persons were murdered by them in this way, for they loved to lap up the warm flowing blood. On one occasion Pierre with his keen white teeth tore out the throat of a girl aged about nine, whom they assaulted in a vineyard. Another time they killed and ate raw a goat belonging to Maître Pierre Bongré.

Other hideous crimes did they confess, and especially that they had frequently covered she-wolves, taking more pleasure in this coupling than in the natural entering of women.

Turbervile, in his *Booke of huntynge*, chapter 75, 1575,[14] tells us : " The Wolfe (sayeth he) goeth on clicketing in February, in such sort as a Dogge lineth a bitch whē she goeth saulte, wherein they abide ten or twelue dayes : many Wolues (where store be) do follow one she Wolfe, euē as Dogges follow a Bitche : but she will neuer be lined but onely with one. She will suffer many to follow hir, and will carrie them after hir sometime eight or tenne dayes without meate, drinke, or rest : and when they are ouerwearied, then she suffreth them all to take their ease, untill they route and be fast on sleepe : & then will she awake yᵉ Wolfe which seemeth most to haue folowed hir, and that oftentimes is the foulest and worst fauourd, bycause he is ouerwearied and lankest : him will she awake and tyce him away with her farre frō the rest, and suffer him to line hir. There is a common Prouerbe,

which saith that : *Neuer Wolfe yet sawe his Syre* : for indeed
it hapneth most comonly that whē all the rest of the Wolues
do awake and misse the female, they follow them by the
sent, and finding them oftentimes togyther, they fall upon
that Wolfe and kill him for despite."

Michel Verdun was discovered upon his attacking, whilst
in the shape of a wolf, a traveller who wounded the animal
which fled into the thicket. Following the trail the gentleman
came to a hut where he found Verdun, who had resumed his
human form, and his wife was bathing the wound.

Associated with Pierre Burgot and Verdun was a third
werewolf named Philibert Montot. All three were duly
executed for their hideous crimes and sorceries, and pictures
of this leash of witches were hung in the Jacobin Church at
Poligny.[15]

A story is related of an incident which occurred about the
year 1530 concerning an old chateau near Poitiers, which
was very ill reputed as the rendezvous of sorcerers and
demons. Three young men, more rash than cautelous,
resolved out of a great curiosity to investigate the matter.
One Friday at midnight they very secretly repaired to the
place, and through the chink of a shuttered window they
were witnesses of the abominations of the sabbat. When
they sought to fly they were beset by three huge wolves.
With difficulty they escaped, and one of them in the fray
Malchused the beast who was biting him. On the following
day it came to his knowledge that a lewd woman of the
town, long suspect of witchcraft, was ill in bed, her ear having
been recently sliced off by a sword.[16]

One of the most famous of all werewolf trials was that of
the loup-garou Gilles Garnier, a native of Lyons, " the hermit
of Dole," as he was called, who was executed at Dole on
18th January, 1573, having been found guilty of the most
hideous sorceries. A contemporary letter, addressed by
Daniel d'Auge to the learned Matthieu de Challemaison,
Dean of the Chapter of Sens,[17] says : " This Gilles Garnier,
the werewolf (*lycophile*), was a solitary who took to himself
a wife, and then unable to find food to support his family
fell upon such evil and impious courses that whilst wandering
about one evening through the woods he made a pact with
a phantom or spectral man, whom he encountered in some

remote and haunted spot. This phantom deluded him with fine promises, and among other gauds eke taught him how to become a wolf, a lion, an ounce, just as he would list, only advising that since the wolf was the least remarkable of savage beasts this shape would be the more conformable. To this he agreed, and received an unguent or salve wherewith he anointed himself when he went about to shift his shape. He died very penitent, having made full confession of his crimes."

The *Arrest memorable de la Cour de parlement de Dole, du dixhuictiesme iour de Ianuier, 1573, contre Gilles Garnier, Lyonnois, pour auoir en forme de loup-garou deuoré plusieurs enfans, et commis autres crimes* was printed at Sens in 1574.[18] This is a document of the first importance.

Anno 1573, on the one part, Henry Camus, Doctor of Laws, Councillor of our Lord the King, in the Supreme Court of the Parliament of Dole, in this case Procurer-General and Public Prosecutor touching the murders committed on the persons of several children and the eating of their flesh in the shape of a werewolf and other crimes and offences committed by Gilles Garnier, a native of Lyons, now held prisoner in the conciergerie of this town, defendant, on the other part.

It is proven that on a certain day, shortly after the Feast of S. Michael last, Gilles Garnier, being in the form of a wolf, seized upon in a vineyard a young girl, aged about ten or twelve years, she being in the place commonly called és Gorges, the vineyard de Chastenoy, hard by the Bois de la Serre, about a quarter of a league from Dole, and there he slew and killed her both with his hands, seemingly paws, as with his teeth, and having dragged the body with his hands and teeth into the aforesaid Bois de la Serre, he stripped her naked and not content with eating heartily of the flesh of her thighs and arms, he carried some of her flesh to Apolline his wife at the hermitage of Saint-Bonnot, near Amanges, where he and his aforesaid wife had their dwelling.

Moreover, eight days after the Feast of All Saints last, again being in the form of a wolf, Gilles Garnier attacked another girl in or about the same place, to wit near the meadow called la Ruppe, in the vicinity of Authume, a spot lying between the aforesaid Authume and Chastenoy, and a little before noon of the aforesaid day, he slew her, tearing her body and wounding her in five places of her body with his hands and teeth, with the intention of eating her flesh, had he not been hindered, let and prevented by three persons. This he has several times freely acknowledged and confessed.

Moreover, some fifteen days after the aforesaid Feast of All Saints, again being in the form of a wolf, having seized yet another child, a boy of ten years old, in a vineyard called Gredisans, at a spot about a league from the aforesaid Dole, situate between the aforesaid Gredisans and Menoté, and having in the same manner as before strangled and killed the aforesaid boy, he ate the flesh of the thighs, legs, and belly of the aforesaid boy, and tore off from the body a leg, dismembering it.

Moreover, upon the Friday before the Feast of S. Bartholomew last he seized a young boy aged twelve or thirteen years under a large pear-tree near the wood which marches with the village of Perrouze in the parish of Cromany, and this young boy he dragged into the said wood, where he strangled him in the same manner as before, with the intention of eating him, which he would have done, had he not been seen and prevented by certain persons who came to the help of the young boy, who was however already dead. The said Gilles Garnier was then and at that time in the form of a man and not of a wolf, yet had not he been let, hindered and prevented he would have eaten the flesh of the aforesaid young boy, notwithstanding that it was a Friday. This hath he freely confessed.

Wherefore this Most High and Honourable Court having carefully considered the plea of the Prosecutor, and having made full inquisition into all depositions and interrogatories touching this present case as well as duly weighing the full and free confessions of the accused, not affirmed and deposed once only but many times unambiguously reiterated, acknowledged and avowed, doth now proceed to deliver sentence, requiring the person of the accused to be handed over to the Master Executioner of High Justice, and directing that he, the said Gilles Garnier, shall be drawn upon a hurdle from this very place unto the customary place of execution, and that there by the aforesaid Master Executioner he shall be burned quick and his body reduced to ashes. He is moreover mulcted in the expenses and costs of this suit.

Given and confirmed at the aforesaid Dole, in the said

Court, upon the eighteenth day of the month of January, in the present Year of Grace fifteen hundred and seventy-three.

The Parliament of Franche-Comté, appalled at the prevalence of lycanthropy in that district, on 3rd December, 1573, issued a special proclamation dealing with the punishment and apprehension of werewolves.[19]

In 1558 occurred a case of werewolfism to which reference is often (but for the most part somewhat incorrectly) made. One evening a landed gentleman, whose château was near a village about two leagues from Apchon in the highlands of Auvergne, met a huntsman whom he knew well and whom he asked to bring him some of the bag on his return. As the huntsman went along a valley he was attacked by a large wolf. Since his arquebus missed aim he was obliged to grapple with the beast which he caught by the ears. By a dexterous feat, however, he managed to draw his keen knife and severed one of the wolf's paws, which he put in his pouch as the beast fled howling. He then took his way back, passing near the gentleman's château, which was actually in sight of the spot where he encountered the wolf. As he told his friend the tale he drew the paw from his pouch, and found therein no paw but a woman's hand with a gold ring upon one of the fingers, a jewel the gentleman immediately recognized as belonging to his wife. With deadly fear in his heart he entered the house to find his wife ill nursing a bandaged arm. When compelled to show her wound it was seen that she had lost a hand, upon which she confessed that in the form of a wolf she had attacked the hunter. Not long after she was burned at Ryon. This was told to Boguet by one who had stayed in that very place a fortnight after the thing had happened, so there can be question as to the actual truth of the occurrence.[20]

There are, indeed, few names more celebrated in the history of witchcraft than that of Henry Boguet of Saint-Claude, Supreme Judge of this district in Burgundy, who in his *Discours des Sorciers* [21] has left us so plain and concise a record of the trials over which he presided, during the epidemic of sorcery—as it may not unfairly be termed—which so grievously infected Burgundy towards the end of the sixteenth century. The bibliography of the *Discours* is extremely complicated, but the issue of the First Edition, which cannot be absolutely determined, is now generally assigned to 1590, and there were at least twelve reprints between that year and 1611. Boguet, honoured and respected by all as the most fearless enemy of the Satanists, died in 1619.

Many of the accused who came before him were guilty of werewolfery, and he devotes chapter xlvii of his *Discours* to an impartial and admirably reasoned discussion *of the Metamorphosis of Men into Beasts, and Especially of Lycanthropes or Loups-garoux*. Since an English translation of his work is readily accessible it will not be necessary here to do more than indicate one or two of the most remarkable cases he was called upon to investigate.

It was in 1584 that Benoist Bidel of Naizan, a lad some sixteen years old, and his younger sister were attacked, whilst plucking wild fruit, by a huge wolf without a tail. Some peasants hastened to their assistance, but the boy had already received his death from the claws and teeth of the animal, which in its turn was killed by those who ran up, and in its last throes crawled behind a thicket, where when it was followed they discovered no wolf but the dead body of Perrenette Gandillon. Soon after, this woman's brother, Pierre Gandillon, and his son George were accused of witchcraft, and it presently came out that they were in the habit of anointing themselves with the Devil's unguent and assuming the form and fierceness of wolves, under which shape they had murdered and eaten many young children. Boguet describes this pair as horrible to look upon, having lost wellnigh any resemblance to humanity, loping on all fours rather than walking upright, creatures with foul horny nails, unpared and sharp as talons, keen white teeth, matted hair, and red gleaming eyes. In the guise of wolves they had frequently attended the sabbat and adored the demon. Both reaped the full reward of their crimes and perished at the stake.

Clauda Jamprost, a wicked old witch, was one of the Orcieres coven, to which crew also belonged Thievenne Paget and Clauda Jamguillaume. All three confessed that by the Devil's aid they had shifted their shape to wolves and haunted the wood of Froidecombe. They used the magic salve, as also did Jacques Bocquet, a werewolf, who was sentenced with them. Clauda Gaillard, a witch of Ebouchoux, likewise guilty of werewolfism, was executed at the same time. Actually Clauda Jamprost was the first to be sent to the stake. She died very penitent. Another witch who was guilty of the same foul offences and suffered the same fate was la Micholette. Françoise Secretain, a notorious witch, who confessed to having attended the sabbat on numberless midnights, to having slain women and children by her craft and killed cattle, to having given herself carnally to the demon who knew her in the shape of a tall black man, was accused of werewolfery by the warlock Jacques Bocquet, but this she did not acknowledge. She was executed in July, 1598.

On the 14th December of the same year at Paris, a tailor of Châlons was sentenced to be burned quick for his horrible crimes. This wretch was wont to decoy children of both sexes into his shop, and having abused them he would slice their throats and then powder and dress their bodies, jointing them as a butcher cuts up meat. In the twilight, under the shape of a wolf, he roamed the woods to leap out on stray passers-by and tear their throats to shreds. Barrels of bleaching bones were found concealed in his cellars as well as other foul and hideous things. He died (it is said) unrepentant and blaspheming. So scabrous were the details of the case that the Court ordered the documents to be burned.

In the same year, again, a werewolf trial took place at Angers. In a remote and wild spot near Caude, Symphorien Damon, an archer of the Provost's company, and some rustics came across the nude body of a boy aged about fifteen, shockingly mutilated and torn. The limbs, drenched in blood, were yet warm and palpitating, and as the companions approached two wolves were seen to bound away into the boscage. Being armed and a goodly number to boot, the men gave chase, and to their amaze came upon a fearful figure, a tall gaunt creature of human aspect with long matted hair and beard, half-clothed in filthy rags, his hands dyed in fresh blood, his long nails clotted with garbage of red human flesh. So loathly was he and verminous they scarce could seize and bind him, but when haled before the magistrate he proved to be an abram-cove named Jacques Roulet, who with his brother Jean and a cousin Julien vagabonded from village to village in a state of abject poverty. On 8th August, 1598, he confessed to Maître Pierre Hérault, the lieutenant général et criminel, that his parents, who were of the hamlet of Gressière, had devoted him to the Devil, and that by the use of an unguent they had given him he could assume the form of a wolf with bestial appetite. The two wolves who were seen to flee into the forest, leaving the body of the slain boy whose name was Cornier, he declared were his fellow padders, Jean and Julien. He confessed to having attacked and devoured with his teeth and nails many children in various parts of the country whither he had roamed. As to his guilt there could be no question, since he gave precise details, the exact time and place, where a few days before, near Bournaut, had been found the mutilated body of a child, whom he swore he had throttled and then eaten in part as a wolf. He also confessed to attendance at the sabbat. This varlet was justly condemned to death, but for some inexplicable reason the Parliament of Paris decided that he should be rather confined in the hospital of Saint Germain-des-Prés, where at any rate he would be instructed in the faith and fear of God. It would seem that the wretched creature was a mere dommerer who could hardly speak plain, but uttered for the most part animal sounds. The full details of the case are not clear.[22]

During the early spring of the year 1603 there spread through the St. Sever districts of Gascony in the extreme south-west of France, the department Landes, a veritable reign of terror. From a number of little hamlets and smaller villages young children had begun mysteriously to disappear off the fields and roads, and of these no trace could be discovered. In one instance even a babe was stolen from its cradle in a cottage whilst the mother had left it for a short space safe asleep, as she thought. People talked of wolves ; others shook their heads and whispered of something worse than wolves. The consternation was at its height when the local magistrate advised the puisné Judge of the Barony de la Roche Chalais and de la Châtellenie that information had been laid before him by three witnesses, of whom one, a young girl named Marguerite Poirier, aged thirteen, of the outlying hamlet of Saint-Paul, in the Parish of Espérons, swore that in full moon she had been attacked by a savage beast, much resembling a wolf. (Espérons is now known as Eugénie-les-Bains, owing to the visits of the Empress Eugénie to the warm sulphur baths here. This small spa has about 610 inhabitants.) The girl stated that one midday whilst she was watching cattle, a wild beast with rufulous fur, not unlike a huge dog, rushed from the thicket and tore her kirtle with its sharp teeth. She only managed to save herself from being bitten owing to the fact she was armed with a stout iron-pointed staff with which she hardly warded herself. Moreover, a lad of some thirteen or fourteen years old, Jean Grenier, was boasting that it was he who attacked Marguerite as a wolf, and that but for her stick he would have torn her limb from limb as he had already eaten three or four children.

Jeanne Gaboriaut, aged eighteen, deposed that one day when she was tending cattle with Jean Grenier in her company (both being servants of a well-to-do farmer of Saint-Paul, Pierre Combaut), he coarsely complimented her as a bonny lass and vowed he would marry her. When she asked who his father was, he said : " I am a priest's bastard." [23] She remarked that he was sallow and dirty, to which he replied : " Ah, that is because of the wolf's-skin I wear." He added that a man named Pierre Labourat had given him this pelt, and that when he donned it he coursed the woods and fields as a wolf. There were nine werewolves of his coven who went to the chase at the waning of the moon on Mondays, Fridays, and Saturdays, and who were wont to hunt during the twilight and just before the dawn. He lusted for the flesh of small children, which was tender, plump, and rare. When hungry, in wolf's shape he had often killed dogs and lapped their hot blood, which was not so delicious to his taste as that of young boys, from whose thighs he would bite great collops of fat luscious brawn.

These informations were lodged on 29th May, 1603. Jean Grenier was arrested and brought before the Higher Court on the following 2nd June, when he freely made a confession of the most abominable and hideous werewolfery, crimes which were in every particular proved to be only too true. He acknowledged that when he had called himself the by-blow of a priest he had lied. His father was Pierre Grenier, nicknamed " le Croquant ", a day-labourer of the hamlet

Saint-Antoine de Pizon, which is situate toward Coutras. He had run away from his father, who beat him and whom he hated, and he got his living as best he could by mendicity and cowherding. A youth named Pierre de la Tilhaire, who lived at Saint-Antoine, one evening took him into the depths of a wood and brought him into the presence of the Lord of the Forest. This Lord was a tall dark man, dressed all in black, riding a black charger. He saluted the two lads, and dismounting he kissed Jean, but his mouth was colder than ice. Presently he rode away down a distant glade. This was about three years ago, and on a second meeting he had given himself to the Lord of the Forest as his bond-slave. The Lord had marked both boys on each thigh with a kind of misericorde, or small stiletto. He had treated them well, and all swigged off a bumper of rich wine. The Lord had presented them each with a wolf-skin, which when they donned, they seemed to have been transformed into wolves, and in this shape they scoured the countryside. The Lord accompanied them, but in a much larger shape, (as he thought) as an ounce or leopard. Before donning the skin they anointed themselves with an unguent. The Lord of the Forest retained the unguent and the wolf's pelt, but gave them to Jean whenever he asked for their use. He was bidden never to pare the nail of his left thumb, and it had grown thick and crooked like a claw. On more than one occasion he had seen several men, of whom he recognized some four or five, with the Lord of the Forest, adoring him. Jean Grenier then related with great exactitude his tale of infanticide. On the first Friday of March, 1603, he had killed and eaten a little girl, aged about three, named Guyonne. He had attacked the child of Jean Roullier, but there came to the rescue the boy's elder brother, who was armed and beat him away. Young Roullier was called as a witness and remembered the exact place, hour, and day when a wolf had flown out from a thicket at his little brother, and he had driven the animal off, being well weaponed. It would be superfluous and even wearisome to chronicle the cases, one after another, in which the parents of children who had been attacked by the wolf, boys and girls wounded and in many cases killed, came forward and exactly corroborated the confession of Jean Grenier.

THE WEREWOLF

The Court ordered Pierre Grenier, the father, who Jean accused of sorcery and werewolfism, to be laid by the heels, and hue and cry was made for Pierre de la Tilhaire. The latter fled, and could not be caught, but Pierre Grenier on being closely interrogated proved to be a simple rustic, one who clearly knew nothing of his son's crimes. He was released.

The inquiry was relegated to the Parliament of Bordeaux, and on 6th September, 1603, President Dassis pronounced sentence upon the loup-garou. The utmost clemency was shown. Taking into consideration his youth and extreme ignorance Jean Grenier was ordered to be straitly enclosed in the Franciscan friary of S. Michael the Archangel, a house of the stricter Observance, at Bordeaux,[24] being warned that any attempt to escape would be punished by the gallows without hope of remission or stay.

Pierre de Lancre, who has left us a very ample account of the whole case,[25] visited the loup-garou at S. Michael's in the year 1610, and found that he was a lean and gaunt lad, with small deep-set black eyes that glared fiercely. He had long sharp teeth, some of which were white like fangs, others black and broken, whilst his hands were almost like claws with horrid crooked nails. He loved to hear and talk of wolves, often fell upon all fours, moving with extraordinary agility and seemingly with greater ease than when he walked upright as a man. The Fathers remarked that at first, at least, he rejected simple plain food for foulest offal. De Lancre calls attention to the fact that Grenier or Garnier seems for some reason to be a name not infrequently borne by werewolves.

Jean Grenier told de Lancre that the Lord of the Forest, who was certes none other than the demon, had twice entered his room at the Friary, tempting him, but that he had warded off the evil one by the Sign of the Cross. The hapless youth, tended to the last by the good religious, died in November, 1611.

Nynauld, *De La Lycanthropie*, relates a history of five sorcerers, werewolves, of Cressi, a village not far from Lausanne, who under the forms of wolves stole a child whom they carried to the sabbat, offering the little boy to the demon. They killed this child, quaffed the blood, and cutting the body to pieces, boiled and ate it, using the fat for their ointments. All five confessed, and were burned quick at Lausanne in 1604.

In the same year a peasant of a hamlet near Lucerne, encountering a fierce wolf on a lonely road was attacked, howbeit he defended himself so well that he struck off the animal's front leg. The beast crawled away, but on being followed a woman was discovered bleeding profusely with her arm severed. She was brought to justice and burned.[26]

During the years 1764 and 1765 a fearful monster, commonly known as the Wild Beast of Gévaudan, spread terror throughout France. The *London Magazine*, January, 1765 [27] (21st December, 1764), notes that the wild beast had ravaged several districts, and " a detachment of dragoons has been out six weeks after him. The province has offered a thousand crowns to any persons that will kill him ". He was supposed by some to be a panther or hyena ; others said he was the offspring of a tiger and a lioness. For months this animal panic-struck the whole region of Languedoc, and is said to have devoured more than a hundred persons. Not merely solitary wayfarers were attacked by it, but even larger companies travelling in coaches and armed. Its teeth were most formidable. With its immense tail it could deal swindging blows. It vaulted to tremendous heights, and ran with supernatural speed. The stench of the brute was beyond description. In vain a Royal Proclamation was issued and large rewards offered for its destruction. During one week of June, 1765, it devoured a woman, a child of eight, a girl of fifteen, and a fourth person. With mysterious skill the beast baffled and even spurned its pursuers.

Writing on 1st April, 1765,[28] Grimm remarks : " For several months now the *Gazette de France* has been chronicling exploits of a new kind, for it never misses to give us an extraordinary recital of this ferocious beast in the Gévaudan, and loudly praises the heroic and memorable feats of those who take the field against this monster." In one particular instance a boy named Portefaix—" l'illustre Portefaix " Grimm salutes him with a smile—although only eleven years old, defended four children from the beast. Mr. Anon at once burst forth into a pæan of poetical praise, and gave the world an Epic Poem in two cantos entitled *Portefaix*.[29] This panegyric occupied five and a half pages.

The countryfolk in the Gévaudan district were well assured that the monster was a warlock, who had shifted his shape, and that it was useless to attempt to catch him. One farmer, a well-to-do and much respected man, deposed before a magistrate that on one occasion when he had encountered the beast, which made a prodigious bound through the air, he heard it murmur in human accents : " Convenez que, pour un viellard de quatre-vingt-dix ans, ce n'est pas mal sauter."

Sutherland Menzies [30] quotes the MS. authority " of a learned but anonymous writer " as remarking, " I remember to have seen an engraving in which that animal was represented devouring a girl, and subscribed Lycopardus Parthenophagus, vulgò *La Bête de Gévaudan*. Parthenophagy, or a peculiar delight in the flesh of girls, is an enormity of the lycanthropes and not of wolves ; from which we may infer in what light the people of the Gévaudan regarded that famous beast." After being in vain pursued by thousands of the people, the monster was at last killed by a Monsieur Antoine, porte-arquebuse du Roi.

A belief in the connection between the werewolf and the vampire lingered in Normandy until at least the beginning of the ninenteenth century. If it was seen that any grave in the churchyard was disturbed the peasants thought a werewolf was buried there. Secretly they exhumed the body, cut off the head with a clean hatchet which must never have been used before, and threw the body into a river or into the sea.[31]

In many parts of France, but more especially perhaps in Britanny, *le Meneur des Loups* is a well-known figure. He is generally considered to be a wizard, who when the werewolves of the district have met and sit in a hideous circle round a fire kindled in the heart of some forest, leads forth the howling pack and looes them on to their horrid chase. Sometimes he himself assumes the form of a wolf, but speaks with human voice. Gathering his flock around him he gives them directions, telling them what farm-towns are ill-guarded that night, what flocks, what herds, are negligently kept, which path the lonely wayfarer setting out from the inn is taking.

FRANCE

" I know," says George Sand, writing in 1858, " several persons who at the first faint rising of the new moon have met near the carfax of the Croix-Blanche old Soupison, nicknamed *Démmonet*, walking swiftly along with great giant strides followed in silence by more than thirty wolves."

One night in the Forest of Châteauroux two wayfarers heard at no small distance the howl of a wolf. They lost no time in climbing a tree for safety sake, and from between the foliage of a high branch they beheld to their amaze a clearing before a woodman's hut, where in the plenilune had gathered a countless pack of wolves. The animals uttered a raucous howl when the door opened, the rustic came out and walked among them, patting their heads and speaking to them, after which they dispersed with every sign of content.

Two gentlemen who were crossing a forest glade after dark suddenly came upon an open space where an old verderer was standing, a man well-known to them, who was making passes in the air, weaving strange signs and sigils. The two friends concealed themselves behind a tree, whence they saw thirteen wolves come trotting along. The leader was a huge grey wolf who went up to the old man fawning upon him and being caressed. Presently the verderer uttering a sing-song chant plunged into the wood followed by the wolves. The two gentlemen who witnessed this themselves related the incident to George Sand, and most solemnly swore that they could not possibly have been mistaken.[32]

At the beginning of the nineteenth century " le grand Julien " of Saint-Août, a skilled player on the *musette*, was a well-known " meneu' de Loups ".

In Normandy tradition tells of certain fantastic beings known as *lupins* or *lubins*. They pass the night chattering together and twattling in an unknown tongue. They take their stand by the walls of country cemeteries, and howl dismally at the moon. Timorous and fearful of man they will flee away scared at a footstep or distant voice. In some districts, however, they are fierce and of the werewolf race, since they are said to scratch up the graves with their hands, and gnaw the poor dead bones.[33]

Adolphe D'Assier in his *Posthumous Humanity* [34] has two instances which he terms lycanthropy, although perhaps the

112

term is loosely enough used. About the year 1868 at Saint-Lizier an animal like a calf suddenly appeared in a room where two brothers were sleeping. Adjured in the name of God it seemed to pass through the door and could be heard on the staircase. The house-door was found fast locked in the morning, and the elder boy always maintained that the appearance was that of a man living in the town who was under no light suspicion of werewolfery.

At Serisols, in the Canton Sainte-Croix, lived a miller named Bigot, a reputed warlock. One morning his wife rose early leaving him asleep in bed, and proceeded to the yard to busy herself with some washing. In a corner of the yard she presently espied an animal something larger than a dog. Seizing the wooden beetle she flung it with all her force, hitting the beast in the eye. At the same moment Bigot awoke in his bed, shrieking out, "Wretch, you have blinded me." Since then he always wore a shade over one eye. This incident was attested by his own children as happening in the year 1879.

Baring-Gould, in 1863, found that after dark nobody dared to cross the plain near Champigni (Vienne), because of a loup-garou who infested that spot, "His tongue hanging out, and his eyes glaring like marsh-fires ! " [35]

In November, 1925, a curious case of werewolfery occurred in Alsace, where the *garde-champêtre*, or village policeman, of Uttenheim, near Strasburg, was tried for shooting dead a boy, who had mischievously worked upon his belief that he was haunted by animals with human faces. He knew that on many occasions the boy had played tricks upon him, but he declared his conviction that, by means of sorcery, the lad had acquired the power of turning himself into the forms of other animals. This was firmly credited by the whole village, and I for one am not prepared to deny that by some glamour, just as Jean Grenier of old, this young lad owing to an impious pact may have been initiated into the dark and horrid secrets of werewolfery.